PLANET JUPITER

Jane Kurtz

PLANET JUPITER

Greenwillow Books
An Imprint of HarperCollins Publishers

Planet Jupiter
Text copyright © 2017 by Jane Kurtz

The text of this book is set in Versailles 45 Light
Book design by Sylvie Le Floc'h

The verses at the beginnings of chapters are from some of the folk songs Jupiter knows and sings while she's busking. Folk songs change often, because they're sung by lots of different people who might have heard words differently or might change them to suit their way of singing. This kind of music travels many a mile over time, and from one continent to another. When someone writes down a verse of such a song, that's just one version. If you'd like to see for yourself, you can easily find on the internet clips of performers singing most of the songs in this book—but you'll see that words and tunes aren't always the same from video to video.

Since I spent most of my childhood in the countryside of Ethiopia, I didn't have a radio for listening to music, so I often sang with my sisters and my dad (who had a lot of cowboy traditions in his background but wasn't a rambler). Now my siblings and I get together every week to sing for our mom. My brother, Chris Kurtz, makes up songs with the third graders he teaches and the Portland bridge song is one of those.

The poem that's referred to on pp. 34 and 64 is "The Moose," by Elizabeth Bishop (from *The Complete Poems, 1927–1979*)

Library of Congress Cataloging-in-Publication Data is available.
ISBN 978-0-06-056486-5 (trade ed.)

17 18 19 20 21 CG/LSCH 10 9 8 7 6 5 4 3 2 1
First Edition

Greenwillow Books

For international families everywhere,
especially my own best-beloveds,
Hiwot, Ellemae, and Noh

PLANET JUPITER

Chapter One

Hangman, hangman, slack your rope.
Slack it for a while.
I think I see my mama coming,
Traveling many a mile.
Mama did you bring me silver?
Did you bring me gold?
Or did you come to see me
Hanging from the gallows cold?

For nine wet and moldy months, my big brother Orion and I had been singing the hangman song. The words were gruesome but ever since we got stuck in rainy Oregon—with no way to get on the road again—I couldn't get enough of songs that were in a minor key and, better yet, gruesome.

My parents named me Jupiter, and I was born to be a street performer, traveling to where there was adventure and busking. I wasn't born to be stuck here, crammed with Mom and Orion into one room on the second floor of Madam Marie's house doing Rainbow Farm chores every day. And today's chore was one of the worst.

Blackberries.

In Oregon, they grew so fierce they had been known to cover up entire tractors.

Orion put on his gloves and saluted the brambles with his loppers. I stood beside him in the drizzle and gave the thorny mess the stink eye. "After today," I said. "I'm never going to chop a blackberry cane again."

He didn't say anything—just started to work, demolishing canes that were way over my head. His boots squelched in the mud. I stomped twice on the muddy ground, and it quivered. "Planning to help anytime soon?" Orion asked.

Huh.

Maybe he wanted to please Madam Marie, who owned Rainbow Farm and who handed out chores the way tourist places handed out brochures.

Maybe we did owe her a thank you.

But seriously? Orion and I should be in California

right now running down sand dunes, watching geckos and busking at a farmers' market. Like normal kids.

I put on my gloves and used the clippers to chomp down on a big cane. Good one! I flung it onto the pile. Drops of water flung themselves back.

"Watch it!" Orion said.

"You watch it," I said. Orion was sixteen. I was eleven. It almost wasn't a fair fight.

I kept grabbing canes with my leather fingers and chomping them off, but his mood was making me uneasy.

Three years ago, my life was a perfect orbit. I, Jupiter, whirled through the universe with four other bodies—a dad with a wild red beard who sang ghosty ballads at night and always made our travels fun. A mom who got obsessed with various stringed instruments and could build houses. Orion, always beside me like a loyal, rumply dog.

And then there was Topher.

I used to think Topher could fix anything—or tell me anything I was itching to know. About animals or plants or what to put on a cut or scrape. He'd grown up next door to Mom in San Francisco, where he and Mom and Mom's sister put together a garage band, and he still lived right there. Whenever we really needed help, he would drop everything and come rescue us. He had the superpower of always being able to fix the old converted school bus we called Paddy Wagon, our trusty vehicle that we slept in and used to haul our supplies.

But Topher was the whole reason we got stuck at Rainbow Farm.

Raindrops started hitting the blackberry leaves and dribbling down my neck.

Three years ago, my dad headed out to have even grander adventures. I missed him, but Mom said a rolling stone just *had* to eventually roll. Anyway, I was pretty sure he would come back someday, and in the meantime he sent us postcards. Fifteen so far.

Chomp. Chomp.

About the same time, my brother turned into a teenager. Instead of a loyal dog, he became more like a coyote—skinny and self-confident with a laughing mouth.

Chomp. Chomp.

But my orbit still kept humming along until late last August when Mom was driving Paddy Wagon from town to Rainbow Farm and it broke down. We had just started brainstorming about how to keep heading south to California when—pow!—suddenly Topher turned into a shooting star, zooming back to San Francisco, leaving the rest of us behind in a place that was soggy even in *May*. How could he have come up with such a dumb, disloyal, awful idea? When Mom said no, he packed up his stupid tightrope and left us in the lurch without even saying good-bye.

"Hey, Jupiter," Orion said, moving close. Drops of water were hanging from his hair. "Which is worse? Chopping blackberries outside where it's cold and wet or chopping onions inside where it's warm and dry?"

Mom and Orion were on kitchen duty tonight. "Worse to be you," I said. "Sorry."

He reached over and tugged my ponytail. "You're pretty good chopping onions," he said.

"Uh-huh," I said. I rescued my ponytail. He and I might be buddies, but that didn't mean I wanted to be stuck with chopping onions.

Orion picked up a shovel and started excavating a root, making sucking sounds in the spring mud. "The kitchen has great acoustics," he said. "We can sing."

Now he was talking. I couldn't wait to be all lit up like a sparkler, wandering down a sunny street with the blue sea shining and our voices in sweet, sweet harmony.

But still no.

Cruunch.

I tugged a tall, prickly cane, and it whipped around and scratched me good.

Ouch!

"Poor Jupiter." Orion leaned on his shovel and gave me a coyote grin. "If you were eighty times more massive you could be a star. Maybe you could be part of my constellation."

"Poor Orion." I sighed dramatically. "Made up of lowly stars while I am a planet." I pulled off one of my gloves and started unhooking thorns.

He shook his damp hair. "Orion has some of the brightest stars in the universe," he said. "Blue and red supergiants."

"Ha-ha," I said.

Mom and Dad gave us big names because they knew they would never give us expensive presents—but who needed things that would only wear out and break? They gave us the ocean, and dolphins, and whales, and fish sizzling over a fire for breakfast.

Would Dad have put up with getting stuck at Rainbow Farm?

Never! Dad was the Prince of Adventure. I wiped my runny nose on my sleeve.

"Nice," Orion said. The root he was fighting poked out like an overgrown troll. "Got a proposition for you," he said, panting. "You help me chop onions tonight. Mom can take your kitchen duty tomorrow night."

"Why don't you want to work with Mom?" I asked. Rainbow Farm had thirty-two artists and musicians and hippies camping in the north pasture, trading work for meals. Thirty-two people ate a *whole* lot of onions.

"She borrowed Madam Marie's car and drove into town." Orion glanced at me. "Not sure she's back yet."

Seriously? Mom never went to town. "Hey!" I said. "She's getting supplies, isn't she? For the road."

Orion wiped his forehead, leaving a muddy streak. "Let's not jump the gun," he said. "Tourists don't flock to the Oregon coast in the rainy months, you know."

Tourists were how we buskers made our money. "We should get to some beach and start figuring things out," I said. "How to get to festivals and things without Paddy Wagon. How to amaze and delight the crowds this year."

"Yeah," Orion half sighed, half whistled. "Paddy Wagon is definitely still broken down."

"Have you considered this, O my brother?" I asked. "Paddy Wagon will stay broken down until we can pay for the repairs." No more Topher fixing it for free. "But we can take a bus to the coast. It won't be long before we're raking in the dough."

"What about school?" Orion asked.

"What about it?" Dad always said no to putting school before adventure—since education could be found everywhere. We'd left school early before. What was *up*?

"I thought you might want to finish out fifth grade with your friends," Orion said.

"Nope," I said. Seriously? As I hummed and clipped and tossed, I was 365 million miles from the Earth, trying to dodge space debris that looked a lot like onions. They all had to be chopped up every time we had lentil soup.

Crunch.

Vegetarian chili also takes lots of onions.

Crunch.

Chickpea curry takes lots of onions.

So do omelets and stew.

Crunch, crunch, *crunch*.

Hacking up that many onions will make you cry even if, technically, you're in a great mood. When we were out of here, I would miss pumpkin-onion cheesecake, though. You use sweet spring onions, and it is actually delicious.

One of the canes stuck out of the pile like a weird, prickly tree. If ants were walking by, they'd think it was as giant as a redwood tree was to me.

The redwoods!

Summer stretched out like a vast and thrilling Milky Way. By fall, Paddy Wagon would be fixed and we'd head back to California, traveling Highway 101, following the footsteps of my dad, the Prince of Adventure. The good life was so close, I could almost stick out my tongue and lick it.

Now if I could only figure out what Orion wasn't telling me.

Chapter Two

If I had known before I'd courted
What all your lying could have done,
I'd have locked my heart in a box of golden
And never would have courted none.

I wiped my wet pruners on my pants and grinned at my brother. "All right," I said. "I'll help with the onions. One last time."

"Thanks," Orion said. "Let's hang it up for the day."

We waded through weeds to the gravel road, and started walking back to the house.

Dad's most recent postcard was a picture of a blind mole-rat. Ugly—like a fat sausage with teeth. The day after we got it, I hopped on a school computer to see if I could figure out what was on Dad's mind. Blind mole-rats spend their whole lives in tunnels. They never see their parents or brothers or sisters, but they communicate through underground vibrations.

Our family had some kind of weird communication system, too, and I usually knew what Orion was up to. "Don't be mad," he said, bumping me.

"I'm not mad," I said. I never got mad. I was one cool cucumber.

In the last nine months, Orion and I had gotten to know every turn and twist in this road. The school bus huffed along here. We walked this way to pick up groceries for Madam Marie and check out the thrift store. "I'm not halfway gone," I sang. "Not just a little bit gone. I'm gone, gone, gone." I kicked gravel in Orion's direction.

"Watch it, Green Bean," he said.

Green Bean? O my brother, how low can you go?

He knew I hated that nickname now. Because I got it from Topher, who had asked Mom and Dad, "Are you really going to give the name of the mightiest planet to a little green bean like that?"

Topher used to be a good guy and my fellow fan of

National Geographic magazines. Why did he have to get the dumb, disloyal, awful idea that he and Mom should get married and maybe even settle down?

I walked faster.

Mom was already married. To Dad. Her heart was locked—like the song says—in a box of golden. And nobody wanted to settle down.

"Earth to Jupiter," Orion said, catching up with me.

"Are you the Hubble telescope?" I asked.

He put his arm over my shoulder and started singing, "Hangman, hangman slack your rope." I jumped right into the harmony, thinking about how sibling voices sound spooky-great together. By next week, we'd be plopping our lucky hat on the sidewalk so people could sling money into it.

We knew how to make a song long or short, depending on the audience. Today we stretched it out while we cleaned the tools and hung them up in the barn—every possible gruesome verse about the maiden who's going to hang, and her mama and papa and brother and sister all refusing to save her from the gallows cold.

Folk songs remind you how tough life can be.

As we stepped out of the barn, I heard cello music drifting from the upstairs of the farmhouse.

Mom was back!

But what was that thing she was playing? It was weird and sad and nothing like her Irish jigs.

I poked Orion. "You don't think she saw Topher in town, do you?"

Orion didn't answer.

Uh-oh. "You don't," I said. "Do you?" I stared up at him with full-on eyeballs. Coyotes can definitely be sneaky. Instead of digging their own dens, they take over from badgers or foxes and move in. But Orion and I never kept secrets from each other. We knew the sounds of each other's snoring and exactly how much singe each of us liked on a marshmallow.

Orion fake-coughed. "You know, we don't actually have a dog in this fight."

What? That was something people said when they didn't care who won a football game. It didn't apply one bit.

"Maybe"—Orion gave me full eyeballs back—"we

need to let Mom make up her own mind about her own life. Maybe—"

"Stop." I pushed him. We did too have a dog in the fight. I opened my mouth but for a long scary minute I couldn't make a sound come out. *Meet my tongue, O my brother. Meet my tonsils. Hide, hide from the wrath of Jupiter.*

I started to run toward the house. Mad, mad, mad.

Chapter Three

I leaned my back up against an oak.
Thinking it was a trusty tree.
But first it bent and then it broke
So the one I love proved false to me.

Orion hollered after me, "Maybe we need—"

No! Dad and I were the type to sing I-don't-need-nobody songs. I pounded through the yard, all hustle and no plan except I knew that if Topher was upstairs with Mom, I had to get him back *out*. When I reached the porch, I bent over with my hands on my knees, catching my breath and listening to the cello's strange song.

Every summer, Madam Marie opened the north pasture to artists and musicians. "Create something beautiful," she always said. "All I ask is a little help with the goats and chickens and such." The day we'd arrived at Rainbow Farm, I never dreamed I would soon know the tiny room on the second floor of this house the way a crab knows its shell.

I started up the steps. One. Two. Slow. Like Mom's cello.

The porch creaked. After Topher left us high and dry—or, technically, high and wet—Madam Marie invited us to stay in the house and even helped Orion and me sprinkle blessed thistle around the house to make sure Topher stayed away.

"Is this scientific?" Orion had asked. I could tell he was trying not to be disrespectful.

"I only wish I had boldo leaf." That's what Madam Marie said. "Boldo leaf really fends off bad characters."

I eased the door open and slid inside. Today, Madam Marie was reading tea leaves. Tea leaves aren't magic. But when they've touched your lips and mixed with your breath, they have *you* in them.

I crept down the hall trying not to disturb the energy. The living room was sea green and gold and spun with crystals and sea stars. Madam and her customer were blocking the stairs. A month ago I'd asked Madam to read my tea leaves, and she'd said she could see Topher there.

"You must be seeing the past," I'd said. "Topher was around a *lot* in the past." In fact, Orion says the night I refused to be born, Topher came with his car and drove Mom and Dad to a hospital. After I was born, Topher and Orion brought three dozen shiny black mussels in a pail to the room, and my brother cried when he found out I couldn't eat any.

Now I was suddenly scared that Madam Marie had read those tea leaves right, after all. What if she'd seen Topher sneaking back in to try again with Mom? My chest felt like I had something wild trapped in there.

Madam Marie moved her index finger along the rim of the cup. "Close your eyes," she said to her customer. "Concentrate on the thought that anything and everything is possible."

I concentrated fiercely on the thought that I *had* to get up the stairs.

Sure enough, Madam Marie turned and saw me. "See only with your inner eye," she crooned to her customer. She waggled her fingers to say *Come. Quick.*

"Is someone up there with Mom?" I mouthed the words as I passed her. "Did Topher—"

She pulled me so close her breath tickled my ear. "Your cousin," she whispered.

What? I shook my head. There had never been cousins in my orbit. As I moved quickly and quietly up the stairs, I heard her say, "One more minute. Then we have a look."

Mom did have an older sister. Amy. When Mom was seventeen, they decided their Balboa Hollow neighborhood was too small to hold them, so Mom went off to play bass guitar in a band, and Amy went off to Africa and said the world would be her family from now on. They burned incense and released each other into the wide and beautiful arms of the universe, and never saw each other again. Not even when Mom went to San Francisco for their parents' funerals.

Dad had never mentioned his family or growing up.

It was hard to imagine the Prince of Adventure doing homework or getting sent to bed.

At the top of the stairs, I paused.

Orion. I sent him a mind message. *Come help me figure out what weirdness is happening here.*

I eased open the curtain that blocked off our room. Mom was bent toward me with her short hair—silver and blue—swinging. I could see the muscles in her wood-chopping, house-building bow arm. Her left fingers fluttered.

No snakes in the burrow, I thought.

Then I saw the girl. Not far from Mom, lying on her stomach, coloring a picture. Maybe seven years old.

Definitely not my cousin!

When she saw me, she pressed her lips tight, scooched closer to Mom, and went back to work.

The main interesting things about the girl were little braids with beads on the ends, and the brown color of her skin that made me think of a fancy seashell. She had a shoebox beside her and a semicircle of colored pencils fanned out in front of her.

My colored pencils.

Mom hated interruptions when she was playing. I took a step toward the girl. A paper lay beside her with the same sentence written all over it.

My name is Edom and I'm from Ethiopia.

What?

Mom's song dropped low. The end . . . except just then, instead, the cello sang out one last high, sad note. Mom relaxed her bow arm and smiled at me. "I haven't played Bach in forever," she said.

"Madam Marie thinks that girl is my cousin," I whispered.

"That's right," Mom said softly. She reached for a piece of paper on her music stand. "Amy wrote it all out for me here. It turns out she met Edom's mom a long time ago in a refugee camp. When Edom's mom died, Amy adopted Edom."

Huh. My brain went *blub blub blub* like a balloon leaking air under water. If someone was adopted, were they a real cousin? "And . . . she came here from Africa?" I asked.

"I know. It's all so unexpected!" Mom unfolded the paper and read: "'A few months ago, I got a tough diagnosis and decided California was my best bet for treatment. I desperately need help to figure out how Edom can have a warm and safe place to call home while I'm going through chemo.'"

Edom didn't say anything. She picked up a fistful of pencils and squirmed herself and her paper over until she was almost behind Mom's chair.

Chemo meant cancer, right? Was Aunt Amy going to die? I had thousands of questions.

Mom kept reading. "'Don't worry. My doctors say I'll be fine soon. My only worry is Edom.'"

How did Edom get to Oregon? And . . . it was all very sad but, seriously? What could we do to help? We were squished in one room and about to get on the road again.

"Does she know any English?" I wasn't sure why I was whispering.

"She wasn't ready to have a conversation yet. I didn't know what to do until the fifth suite sarabande came soaring out of my memory."

Mom could fill a room with tenderness just by touching horsehair to strings made out of goat guts.

Now she leaned down toward Edom. "Are those elephants?"

"Elephants make sense," I told Mom. "She probably saw a lot of elephants in Ethiopia."

Edom looked up. "Don't be ignorant," she said.

Chapter Four

Love, oh love, oh careless love
Love, oh love, oh careless love
Love, oh love, oh careless love
You see what love has done to me

So rude! I tried to catch Mom's eye to whisper, "Seriously?" but she was still looking sweetly at Edom.

I'd never spent much time with other kids. One day, I came home from school and told Mom and Orion that the planet Jupiter keeps sixty-seven known moons spinning around it—more moons than any other planet in the solar system, and Orion had said, "And that planet has nothing on the Jupiter we know and love." It's true. No matter where I go to school, I get along with everyone, even substitute teachers. But once the afternoon bell rings, I never hang around.

And here was a kid who was supposed to be my cousin soaking up all of Mom's attention.

I did know that questions are not always welcome. Everyone has a right to keep things private. That's what Mr. Isaacs, my second-grade teacher, said when kids were chasing me around asking, "Where do you live? Where do you live?" and I didn't feel like telling them about Paddy Wagon and all.

Outside, a dog barked. Serena. I heard Zeb-the-beekeeper call, "That dog lives to supervise!"

"She's the expert," Orion called back. "Too bad she can't come inside and organize the kitchen."

Orion and I had found Serena hiding by a log off the gravel road. It took us a lot of work to convince that collie pup that she needed a home and to convince Zeb he needed a dog.

Half the time, Orion acted like Serena was *his*.

"Gotta go," I told Mom and lit out, clattering down the stairs. Whatever my brother knew about this, he'd better spill.

Madam Marie was at the door saying good-bye to her customer. "Zeb tells me he senses the ghost of a wandering cow in one of the back fields," she said as I rushed by.

In the kitchen, I palmed an onion and gave it a stab with a knife. A sour-and-earth smell whooshed up.

Orion came in and took up his position beside me. "I know what you're going to say." He slid the skin off an onion.

I didn't say anything.

"Mom did see Topher in town. I should have told you." He sliced the onion in two. "But she said he would be right back out of our lives again immediately."

I swiped at my eyes with the back of my hand. Dang onions!

"Mom's soft heart took over when she saw the poor kid, huh?" Orion's knife went *tick tick tick* through the onions. "Zeb told me he saw them get out of the car together."

I pointed my knife upstairs. "That poor kid sure knows English perfectly for someone who's supposed to be an Ethiopian orphan."

"Don't be a meanie, Beanie."

Great. Now I was ignorant and mean. "Did you and Mom make some plan *without me?*" I asked. "Because that would just be *wrong.*"

"Not at all." Orion rocked his knife like a pro. "Mom only agreed to sit down with Topher and try to figure something out for Edom."

"So Topher has someone new to rescue," I said. "Good for him."

"He knows a guy who owns a small house in Portland," Orion said. "It's going to be torn down so a bigger house can go on that lot. But while stuff is being worked out, the owner won't charge rent."

"So he and Edom are going to live in Portland?" I started chopping faster. It wasn't as if I cared—only that I'd gotten used to Topher traveling with us, starting the night Dad left. Mom had wrapped her arms around us and said, "Your dad is the bravest and best Prince of Adventure. I knew when I married him that he was a rolling stone that would gather no moss, but he gave us this amazing life, didn't he?" Mom and Orion and Topher and I spent the evening throwing Mom's collection of sea glass toward the moon and sending good wishes to Dad on his journeys.

"Hang on," Orion said. "Hang with me, here. Topher has been working on a mural in San Francisco all winter and he's got to get back and finish it."

All winter while mold was growing on me in Oregon, Topher was painting sunshine in California and not missing us one bit. My eyes were stinging. "You're being too random," I said. "What's your point?"

"The house in Portland." Orion's voice was impatient. "Get it? He thought maybe Mom could turn it into a temporary home for Edom until Aunt Amy is better."

Wait! *Us* in the house? "But we're getting on the road," I said.

"That was Mom's reaction, too," Orion said. "She must have changed her mind when she saw Edom."

What a weaksauce idea! Mom hadn't spent time in Portland since she went to college there, when she was pregnant with Orion. One time, she drove us through the city to show us. I remembered streets all streaky with rain. Rain falling on the sidewalks and on a flock of bicycles. And why would she disrupt our lives for someone she didn't even know existed until now?

Probably because of what she said that time we were lying on our backs watching geese. Topher said, "All those birds except the leader are flying in the upwash from the wings ahead of them, so the whole team can travel long disances without getting worn out."

Mom stretched her arms to the sky and said, "All for one, and one for all."

She *did* have a soft heart.

"Okay," I said. "But we have to be heading south in five months—tops. Oregon winters are for people who have gills and hair-thin bones."

Orion laughed.

"I'm serious!" I said. "And what if Topher talks Mom into letting him hang around to help out?" I stabbed an onion ferociously. "He better be already gone, gone, gone. I'm asking Madam Marie for blessed thistle. When we get to Portland, you have to help me spread it around the house."

"Yeah, um, the thing is . . ." Orion coughed. "I'm not going with you to Portland."

"What?"

He started talking fast. "I've lined up a job at the Hawk Creek Café. I can move into the old llama stall in the barn."

"No!" I slammed the knife down. "That's ridiculous."

He reached out a hand to ruffle my ponytail, and onion smell flew into my face.

"Is it Serena?" I asked. I could imagine Orion refusing to leave the collie behind. "Because maybe—"

"Poor Jupiter," he said. "Everything's gone wobbly, right?"

Poor Jupiter? I was fuming. *Save your pity for Edom, my brother.* Her story was pathetic.

"You know," Orion said. "Someday I might want to go to college. Maybe I need something normal on my college application. Like a summer job. Jessica said she'd do me a favor and put in a good word for me at the Hawk."

Jessica! I had seen them talking. "You can't," I said. Coyotes loped over the California hills. They didn't work in cafés. I waved my knife desperately. "Don't sell your soul to the settling down."

Orion tried not to laugh, but a snort leaked out.

"It's not funny!" I could feel tears leaking from my eyes because of the dang onions. "Have some self-respect, Orion! A rolling stone gathers no moss— remember? What Dad always says?"

Orion's face had a squiggle of humor and a squiggle of sadness. "Did it ever occur to you, that makes *us* moss?"

"No!" I said. "No it doesn't! Tell me you're joking about staying here."

Orion shook his head.

Just like that, I felt the whole solar system exploding.

Chapter Five

Come all ye fair and tender ladies.
Take warning how you court young men.
They're like a star on a summer's morning.
First they'll appear and then they're gone.

After supper, I wandered around the south pasture howling at the moon. Dad said we should do three brave things a day—preferably before breakfast. I refused to believe my brother would ditch any kind of adventure for some stupid chance to hang around with Jessica.

By the time I went inside, I felt better, but then I saw that Mom had abandoned Orion and me and was going to sleep with Edom in the living room. Wow. What a rotten deal.

The next morning at breakfast Mom redeemed herself, though, when she told us to get everything packed up because we were going to leave Rainbow Farm tomorrow.

Tomorrow!

Looking at Orion across the table, I was sure he would change his mind, especially if Mom let him drive the rental car that Topher had left for Mom to drive to Portland. Edom was stretched out on the bench between Mom and me, with her head in Mom's lap. When I was little, I would do that and Mom would comb my hair with her fingers and tell me stories about when she was pregnant with me. She'd laugh and say no wonder my hair was the color of California sun and sand.

"Can I have some coffee?" Edom asked.

"You're just a kid," I said.

"Amy-mom lets me."

I doubted that. But all Mom said was, "You two store anything in Paddy Wagon that you don't need right away."

I didn't want to ask in front of Edom how long chemo usually took.

Mom was a flop at some things: clipping coupons and writing numbers in a line when they have to be added up the same way twice. But she was great at showing us how to travel light. I focused on organizing my busking clothes and beads. It had been a long time since I'd really had a chance to perform. Even my hair seemed less shiny now—more like the color of the dust the Rainbow Farm chickens took baths in.

I made a giveaway pile, keeping an eye on Orion. He'd better be thinking Portland and not the llama stall.

Finally, I put my most precious things into their zipped bag.

Two fancy shells and half a sand dollar.

A button from an old Dad shirt.

The postcards.

A folded-up moose poem by some famous person that I got to read to the whole school with hundreds of eyes looking up at me. "Show-off," one of the sixth graders had whispered—loud enough for me to hear— but the kid beside her said, "Shh," so what did I care?

When my bags were downstairs, I gathered my stack of *National Geographic*s and the field guide Orion and I used to identify tracks and scat when we camped in out-of-the way places where coyotes and kangaroo rats roamed. I hauled them out to Paddy Wagon.

In the yard, I met up with Mom and Edom. "Hey," I said to Mom. "Can I talk to you? In private?" I stared at Edom for a long hanging-from-the-gallows minute. She didn't budge. After a few seconds, I realized Mom wasn't going to make her, so I said, "Never mind," and walked off. I wasn't mad, but I was seriously annoyed.

Who asked for a kid stuck like a mollusk to my mom?

Even though it was my last day, Madam Marie assigned me a chore—helping set the long tables for supper. Sky Peace counted out the plates and told me, "We're a good team."

Some adults rejected any cup or glass that had a bit of food or something stuck to it. Sky Peace just rubbed it clean with her floaty scarves. The main interesting thing about her, though, was how we'd make each other laugh with our dance moves, like the Robot, which worked perfectly for forks and knives.

Tomorrow . . . *infinite possibilities*. Dad said that

people claim they want adventurous lives, but they start sleepwalking through life and miss the possibilities. One of his postcards was a guy holding an alligator. On the back, Dad had written, "Grab adventure by the tail."

When the supper bell rang, Mom came out of the kitchen laughing and wiping her wet hands on her jeans. Followed by Edom.

I ran upstairs to pull on a fluffy skirt and arm bangles. It was our last supper and I, for one, was going to dress for it.

As Dad wrote on his wolf postcard, "One life to live. The girl. The boy. The myth. The legend."

When bowls of goat stew were being passed around the tables, Zeb-the-beekeeper stood up. "Our community has been lucky to have a resident cello-player all winter," he said. "To say nothing of the dog-loving Orion and the fierce and fabulous Jupiter."

This was our moment!

Zeb went on. "They will be missed, but the family is doing a noble thing."

Everyone clapped.

I jumped to my feet to take a bow, because Orion

and I don't need coaching—we know everything goes better when the cute kids bow.

Being noble felt great! I bowed to the right and left—and then I realized Edom had slid off the bench and onto the floor under the table.

Hey, I thought. Don't wreck our moment.

There went Orion, after her.

Hey, I thought again. Don't leave me out!

I dropped down, leaving Mom to handle the public.

Orion's neck was bent at an awkward angle. "What are we doing?" I whispered. From the sounds of it, people were going back to eating and talking. Our moment was over.

"I don't think Edom likes people staring at her," Orion whispered back.

It was hard not to turn and stare at her. "Maybe because of when she and her mom were all hungry, sitting in the Ethiopian refugee camp," I whispered. There were kids at school who were known for being insensitive, but not me.

"My birth mom and Amy-mom were nurses in the camp," Edom said, not even whispering. She put one hand to her ear and the other on Orion's chest—acting out a stethoscope.

I'm not ignorant, I wanted to say. I know what a nurse is.

"And the refugee camp wasn't in Ethiopia," Edom said. "It was Kenya."

Orion gave me his sideways look. "Better brush up on your geography," he said. "I'll quiz you when we meet up again."

So he really wasn't coming. The skin on my face felt tight—like I'd turned into a naked mole rat being swallowed by a sand boa.

The only thing I could think was, at least mole rats can communicate by head-drumming and jaw-listening even when they're far apart. Maybe that's what Dad's postcard was all about. He knew I'd find a way to let him know if he really, really needed to get back to the burrow.

Chapter Six

I have brought no silver
I have brought no gold.
I have come to see you
hanging from the gallows cold.

The next morning, I had to watch Orion carry his things to the barn with Serena at his heels. It made me feel weird. I was good with good-byes. Still, I'd been with Orion since I wasn't even a day old and he brought me that bucket of mussels—which must have been pretty smelly, I told him at breakfast.

"Mussels are one of the sea's best sources of food," Orion said. "They're easy to gather and high in protein, minerals, and vitamins B_1 and B_2, and extremely tasty."

"What are you," I said. "A brochure?" Maybe he was feeling weird, too. "Say good-bye to anyone at school who asks about me," I added. Not that I cared, really. Anyway, according to Dad, education can't be locked in a classroom. It comes from people. Nature magazines. Animals. Rocks. Stars. Everything.

"You won't let Mom forget there's such a thing as money, right?" Orion said. "That stuff most people trade for food?" He glanced at Edom, who was sitting between us and kept looking around for Mom.

Seriously? "I don't think our money is your beeswax if you're not going to come help."

"How are you going to busk without me?" Orion reached over Edom and squeezed my shoulder.

I pushed my scrambled eggs back and forth. "We'll figure it out. And by the way, I got an A in math. Did you show your report card to the Hawk Creek Café?"

He grinned. "Hey. They hired me for my looks, not to balance the books. They know their beeswax."

Edom leaned forward and talked with toast in her mouth. "The café sells beeswax?"

I left Orion to explain while I carried my bags to the

car. At Rainbow Farm, I'd mostly worn jeans. Thick ones. The kind invented during the Gold Rush. For Portland, I'd packed skirts and leggings. My socks and beads and bangles were in a daypack.

Orion found me and helped carry out a box labeled MISCELLANEOUS, full of handy things like rhythm instruments, out to the rental Toyota. We trudged back and forth. Sleeping bags. Mom's clothes. Madam Marie had packed a basket of sesame cakes and bread with cinnamon and a jar of blackberry jam. We grabbed that last, along with three pillowcases stuffed with what we would need the first night—a system Orion had invented.

"Just two people earning money could be tough," Orion said. He reached down to rub Serena's ears.

"We'll be fine." I noticed he didn't include Edom. She could help.

"Cities take steady income." He had his serious voice on. "Don't forget this is a whole new gig for Mom."

Orion probably had bad memories of being a little kid in Portland. Mom was really young then. "Nothing bad is going to happen," I said.

"Check out the busking laws," he said. "And be smart about your emotions, okay? No Red Spot of Jupiter."

"Ha-ha," I said.

The Great Red Spot is a high-pressure storm on the planet Jupiter that has lasted for at least 300 years, according to scientists who saw it through a telescope. Orion brought it up after Topher left. Okay, maybe I did lose my cool occasionally. But if I did, it was only for a few days.

We stood by the car. Orion had Madam Marie's basket of sesame cakes.

I suddenly wanted something.

I wanted everything.

I lifted the napkin on the basket and took a cake. I stuffed it in my mouth and with the other hand I shoved my brother away.

"What?" He shoved back, a little harder than he probably planned.

Before I knew it, I was flat in the grass with Serena licking my face. I could hear Mom inside the house, laughing. I forced myself to laugh, too, until I was laughing so hard I could hardly stumble to my feet.

"Hey," I said. "Give me the café's phone number so I know how to talk to you."

Instead, Orion began to sing.

"Hangman, hangman, slack your rope.
Slack it for a while.
I think I see my brother coming,
Traveling many a mile."

"Please," I said. "Please, please?"

He put the basket of cakes on the car floor and kept singing.

"Brother, have you brought me silver?
Brother, have you brought me gold?"

I climbed into the back seat. "You're hanging from the gallows cold," I shouted.

He leaned into the car. "I don't have the café number but I'll get it for you. I'll send it with the silver and gold." He rubbed his silly coyote chin against my hair. "Even though you don't have a phone."

Okay. I got it. The song was supposed to remind me that the money from his café job would help us. "You need to quit worrying so much," I said.

Orion backed up. "I'll try," he said. "Mom will definitely turn out to know someone in Portland."

Seriously! Mom always surprised us with her amazing "all for one, and one for all" collection of people. "It's a minor detour on the road to freedom," I said. "I'll bet Dad will hang around with us this summer on the coast."

Orion's eyebrows quirked upward. "Nah," he said. "That guy is gone for good."

"You're wrong!" I shouted.

The farmhouse screen door slammed. Mom was on the porch with Edom, who was clutching her shoebox. I waved good-bye to Madam Marie. She'd given me a jar of blessed thistle for the Portland house.

"Be nice to our cousin," Orion said. "She didn't ask to be here."

And I didn't ask her to be here. In fact, Edom was the whole reason Orion and I would be apart for the first time ever.

"Hug me good-bye?" Orion asked.

I shook my head no. Too, too sad.

"All right," Orion said. "Have it your way."

I closed my car door. Time to get Rainbow Farm in our taillights. *So long, everyone. Out of the way, Orion. We're barreling through.*

When my brother was almost to the porch, I slid the window down. "Good-bye, Orion," I shouted.

Chapter Seven

The minstrel boy to the war is gone.
In the ranks of death, you'll find him.
His father's sword he has girded on
And his wild harp slung behind him.
—*from "The Minstrel Boy," Thomas Moore (1779–1852)*

Mom buckled her cello in the front and buckled Edom in the back with me. I rested my nose on the window, feeling like a tide-pool creature. Orion and I had spent hours watching sea stars and urchins and cucumbers and snails on the bottoms of the pools and dribbling down the rocks. Maybe they were staring up at us through clear water while we were looking down at them.

I was no sea cucumber, I reminded myself. I was the white wolf on Dad's postcard—alone and fierce and free in the middle of a gigantic wilderness. Orion and I would just have to be like Mom and her sister, Amy, who gave each other up to the wide and beautiful arms of the universe.

I didn't need anyone.

"Ready to say later-gator to Rainbow Farm?" Mom asked Edom.

Edom frowned. "That's not the way Amy-mom says it."

Mom laughed and didn't take it personally. Then she started the car.

On the road again! "How did you like your trip to America?" I asked Edom.

"I didn't like it." She frowned. "Amy-mom said I was being big trouble, but I was *not*."

"Oh." I tried again. "Did Amy-mom give you that shoebox? What do you have in it?"

Edom held it to her chest. "It's personal," she said.

Okay.

Mom maneuvered the car expertly around the Rainbow Farm circle and toward the gate. "Where do you think Dad is right now?" I asked.

She glanced back at me, raising her eyebrows over snazzy new sunglasses. "I imagine him . . . I don't know . . . maybe riding camels in North Africa. A blue robe is fluttering up around him, the same color as his eyes."

Wow . . . Africa. Even Highway 101—most amazing coastal highway ever—was probably too small for the Prince of Adventure.

We reached the gravel road. "Not as roomy as Paddy Wagon, is it?" Mom said.

Not roomy at all. "Did you see that fixed-up bus by the barn?" I asked Edom. "Mom's name is Patricia, so when Topher found it for us he named it Patty's wagon. Dad changed it to Paddy Wagon."

"It's not a wagon, though," Edom said.

Dust poofed behind us. "'Paddy wagon' is what people once called the vehicles policemen used for hauling prisoners around," Mom said.

Edom frowned. "It's a prison?"

"It's freedom!" I said. Or it was until it broke down.

"We're off!" Mom loved driving. "If you need to stop, let me know," she said to Edom. "But give me plenty of warning. Unless you don't mind going behind a tree."

"Amy-mom and I went behind lots of trees." Edom looked as stubborn as a clam.

Soon we were sailing down the scenic Pacific Coast Highway, where the ocean reminded me of a wrinkly blue cloth with white fringe. Mist fluffed over a bay and people in fishing boats. Sometimes they didn't want the fish they caught and gave them to someone else—like us.

Edom read signs under her breath. "Can we go to the Sea Lion Caves?"

"It's a dirty, smelly tourist trap," I told her. "You wouldn't like it."

"Why do they trap them?"

I tried hard not to laugh. "It's a word picture," I said. "Not a real trap."

We sailed through towns. Past a church camp where we had once parked a borrowed car because we knew no one would notice it while we lived for a few days on the beach. People think they have to own things, but if you give up that idea, you can really have the sea and constellations and tide pools. You can blend in at camp and eat s'mores and listen to the singing. One night we heard a song about how wolves would lie down with lambs and the fierce would not devour the small.

After that, Orion used to tease me by saying, "Be benevolent, Jupiter. No devouring the small."

I took my postcards out. They all had U.S. postmarks, so maybe Dad was really here on this continent.

Trees were looming on both sides of the road. My teacher liked the moose poem because of the words about fog: salty and thin. But I liked the words about trees. Splintery with mist caught in their branches.

I studied the postcard with a ripe red raspberry on it. *"Jolts of joy are everywhere,"* Dad had written on the back. He was probably remembering the summer he'd decided we should learn to forage for food in a forest, and we'd picked thousands of berries.

Mom buzzed the window down. "Smell the cool delicious, Edom? The air is sweeter when the trees are breathing it."

Foraging didn't always work out. Dad would call Topher when we ran out of supplies, and Topher would meet us at a trailhead and hand over things we needed.

I preferred busking.

As if my thoughts had poked her, Mom started to sing "Rambling Boy," a song she said reminded her of Dad. I tried harmony on the chorus and thought we sounded pretty great. We'd show Orion he didn't need to be working at that café. The thought gave me such a jolt of joy that I looked over at Edom and said, "I like your braids. Especially the beads."

She patted her head as if trying to remember what they looked like. "Amy-mom did them," she said. "Before."

Before what? "Amy-mom and your real mom must have been brave and noble," I said. "I mean helping in a refugee camp and all that."

I stopped. Buskers learn to read expressions.

Edom's expression said, Go eat a ketchup sandwich.

I tried again. "Did you ever ride in cars? Before?"

She frowned. "That *offends* me," she said.

"It does?"

Mom jumped in. "Edom and her mom and Amy shared a house in a city," she said. "Isn't that right?"

Apparently Edom didn't mind talking to *Mom* about personal things.

The trees had started dropping big splats of water and pinecones on the car. My mood called for belting something out! I started in with the minstrel boy in the ranks of death, but Edom interrupted. "Too sad. Stop." She put her hands over her ears. "Stop!"

Okay. She definitely wouldn't like the hangman song. I gave up and practiced juggling my lucky stones while Edom drew. "Did you ever see a picture of Mom when you were in Ethiopia?" I finally asked when I was tired of the silence. "Did you know we existed?"

"No," Edom said. Very softly.

So she was as startled by us as I was by her. And then she must have been shocked to find herself in that car with Topher driving off. "Did you even want to be adopted?" I asked. "After . . ." I stopped.

She didn't look up. "None of your beeswax."

Wow. Zing me! I had to laugh, and even Edom couldn't help a teeny smile. I wanted to ask her if she spoke Ethiopian, but . . . nah.

"What are you working on?" Mom asked.

She held it up, as if Mom had eyes in the back of her head. "It's elephants under the roses," Edom said.

"Interesting," Mom said. "Did you know we're going to be living in the city of roses?"

"Maybe she saw elephants in photographs," I explained. "Maybe she doesn't know how tiny roses are compared to them."

Edom gave me a look of pure scorn.

Around noon, Mom parked at the Tillamook Cheese Factory where the "guided tour" is pretty much just a walk up some stairs so you can look down through windows at the factory floor. I liked it anyway. "Can I meet you at the fake cow in about half an hour?" I asked.

I knew she'd say yes. When people were discussing stranger danger versus free-range kids, everyone knew what Mom and Dad thought. But I was surprised when she said, "You go with her, Edom." She turned to me. "Keep a very close eye on her. I want to see if I find any bargains. And take her to the bathroom in case my tree technique isn't up there with Amy's."

Edom looked panicked.

Mom gave her a gentle push. "Stick right with Jupiter. She knows to use her noodle at all times."

She tapped Edom's head. "That's your noodle."

The Tillamook Cheese Factory didn't need a noodle. It was full of families and . . . ice cream. But, okay. I'd teach Edom—like Orion, a long time ago, had taught me.

As I started off, Edom glanced back at Mom with worry lines pinching her eyebrows together. "It's okay," I told her. "Adults on vacation are almost always in a good mood. For example, when we pulled over to see gray whales migrating, people would sometimes talk to us for ten minutes straight."

She reluctantly let me lead her to the ladies' room. "It's easy to spot helpful people," I told her. "See that mom over there?"

Going up the stairs, I showed her how you can fall in behind a family and seem part of the group. "Or see that guy taking a picture of those kids?" I asked. "A grandpa. Right?"

No matter how benevolent I was, Edom looked like a grumpy elephant seal.

When we got in line for the cheese samples, though, she crammed up close. What were people thinking— me with my sandy hair and blue eyes, and Edom with her brown skin and braids? "By the way," I told her, "I don't really get how you're my cousin."

Edom was reading the sign about cheese fun facts. "When sisters have kids," she said, "the kids are cousins."

Yeah. I knew what cousins were. I tried a different approach. "It must have been weird becoming Aunt Amy's kid when she was just your friend before," I said.

Edom looked down at the floor. Then she said, "After I got born, Mom and Amy-mom took turns traveling because they worked for Doctors Without Borders."

"Oh," I said. "They went to different places where people needed nurses?" Aunt Amy was probably like Mom and liked new scenes.

"Then there was an outbreak or something," Edom said. "They both went. To help. I stayed in Ethiopia with my grandma."

"But—"

"My mom didn't come back." Edom's voice got low and sad. My breathing was stuck. Then she said in a rush, "And Amy-mom adopted me."

"I think I get it." I said. "You mean because . . ."

She nodded, so I didn't say it but I thought it.

Edom's mom died trying to help other people.

Wow. I was spinning too fast for my orbit. Her mom never should have gone, I thought fiercely.

But then if the doctors and nurses didn't help, some people wouldn't have anybody.

Wow.

Right then I decided I would always be nice to Edom.

Always.

Chapter Eight

The train I ride on
Is a hundred coaches long.
You can hear her whistle blow a hundred miles.
If this train runs me right
I'll be home tomorrow night.
I'm nine hundred miles from my home.
And I hate to hear that lonesome whistle blow.

As we finished up at the Tillamook Cheese Factory, I couldn't get over how unfair it was that Edom's mom died and now Amy-mom was sick, like some sorrowful, lamenting song full of torment and woe. My benevolent feelings lasted all the way to lunch, when I spread our samples out on a picnic table and showed Edom how cheese curds squeak when you bite down on them. I thought she'd smile but she wrinkled her nose as if the sound was disgusting.

Mom had gotten three long pepperoni sticks. "Two feet of pepperoni for a dollar!" she said.

"What is it?" Edom held hers up.

"Pepperoni?" Mom waved hers like a conductor's wand. "It's like sausage. Pork or beef, and garlic and fennel and mustard seeds, and things like that."

Edom poked it cautiously. "Is it pork or beef?"

Mom didn't say, "Never say *ew* to food." Instead, she said, "I'm not sure."

It was like my real mom had gotten sucked into a black hole.

Edom scratched at the plastic wrapping with her fingernail, and then she put hers in her shoebox. Maybe she was a vegetarian, but a traveling family can't handle picky eaters.

Back in the car, I showed Edom how to make origami birds. While we smoothed and folded the paper, I thought about Dad. Maybe he was in Alaska . . . on a fishing boat . . . or . . . I should remind Mom that they used to say we would never live in a city where light pollution is so bad that people can't see the stars and planets. "We don't want any celestial beings losing their way," Mom would say, wrapping us all in a hug.

"You know," Mom said to Edom, "I want to hear all about Amy. What can you tell me?"

"Like what?" Edom asked.

"Like . . ." Mom paused. "So much. Let me think."

How had someone like Mom actually said good-bye forever to her sister? Did she ever feel hollowed out and broken open? My whole life, when I was hungry or scratched up or so tired I had to crawl, I'd always had Orion to help me figure things out.

The car felt way too empty without him.

We pulled around a truck full of huge logs. "My mom met my dad when she was building a log cabin and she was only seventeen," I told Edom.

Mom laughed. "How often does someone roll into your life who is a wizard with a chainsaw and knows hundreds of songs? Not to even mention the red hair and blue eyes and flannel shirts."

She'd always said Dad told her right away that he wasn't the staying kind, and she said she was lucky he stayed a lot longer than he'd planned, and he left behind the two things she'd always pack up and take with her—a constellation and a planet.

This time she didn't say it, though, maybe because this time she didn't pack the constellation.

Outside the window, I saw NATHANIEL, WE WILL ALWAYS LOVE YOU painted on a camper by the side of the road like a small mysterious story. And then—"Look!" I read the sign out loud: "Ocean Front Property for Sale." The arrow pointed down a side road. "Can we? Please?"

If you park your car behind an empty house and wander down to the beach, you can find free mussels and sea beans for supper. You can make a pillow of sand. Orion and I would watch wriggling waves while Mom chanted the names of the Portland bridges she used to ride her bike over at night. "Maybe," she said now.

"No big deal to finish the trip tomorrow," I said. Dad would *never* miss a last chance to sleep at the beach.

"What do you think, Edom?" Mom asked.

"No!" Edom gave me a clammed-up look of stubborn meanness.

"Please?" I put on my most imploring voice. Mom would understand. She was my *mom.*

"No!" Edom kicked the back of the seat.

"It's okay," Mom said. "We'll find a place to turn off and take one last walk and show Edom a little bit of the Oregon coast."

Not okay. Mom parked, but all she and Edom did was walk cautiously along the sand. I ran ahead, flinging rocks into the water and screeching with the seagulls. Being nice was already getting old. Aunt Amy's chemo had better finish up.

Fast!

Chapter Nine

Portland bridges across the Willamette, deep and wide.
Taking everybody on over to the other side.
Driving across the river at night
Flying through a city of light.
Portland bridges across the Willamette, deep and wide.

When we were back in the car and driving again, my old life peeled away.

New places are like eating something unexpected. You have to roll things around in your mouth for a while. Also, new places are like skateboarding down a mountain. You're tucked in. Wheels rumbling. Laughing because it's scary and exciting all at the same time. Infinite possibilities.

That's the part Dad loved.

It didn't take long before we were in civilization—small towns with coffee shops and thrift stores. Orion and I could always make each other laugh in thrift stores. A pink hat, a fake fur jacket, a beaded scarf. Sometimes we found things we truly loved, too, including a tiara and a pair of black-and-pink tights that I wore to school in California every day for a month one year.

Luckily, Mount Hood poked out of the horizon like a promise of adventure. The thought made me happy until rain started coming down like a curtain, and cars surrounded us.

"I've had years to wonder things about Amy," Mom said. "Does she still sing all the time? Jupiter, my sister could lay down a gorgeous tenor line." She didn't let Edom answer before other questions tumbled out. Did Amy still wear red shoes? Did she get a chance to climb Mount Kilimanjaro? Did she ever kayak down the Zambezi River? "She told me not to worry," Mom added, "because she could pop any crocodile over the head with her paddle."

Edom giggled—and then instantly got serious. "She has to be in bed," she said.

"I know," Mom said. Softly. "But she'll be stronger soon."

"How did Amy-mom know how to find us?" I asked.

"Lucky thing Topher still lives in Balboa Hollow, where he and Amy and I grew up, right Edom?" Mom gave Edom a warm glance in the mirror as if the two of them were sharing a special secret.

Which, technically, they were. Mom and Amy and Topher were in that garage band together and all. How come *I* never got to see that neighborhood?

The whole thing made me want to change the subject. Fast.

"I got to read a poem in school," I said. "It was about a bus full of people and suddenly there was a moose stepping out from the trees and looming in the middle of the road. Wouldn't that be great right here? Something weird and unexpected?"

"Whoa, Nellie," Mom said. "It would get squashed."

"Who's Nellie?" Edom asked.

Mom had picked up strange vocabulary as she and Dad had gigged and hammered from California to Canada.

"It doesn't mean anything," I said. "It's an expression."

Edom frowned. "If things don't mean anything, why do people say them?"

Mom laughed. "When we were kids, Amy and I would say, 'Oh, popcorn!' Does Amy still say that?"

I gave up and went back to my postcards. On one of them, a girl with blond braids was picking flowers, and a space monster had landed right behind her, but she was oblivious. *Notice everything.* Dad had written on the back. *Get the lay of the land.*

Edom handed me an origami bird. "Can we sell them?" she asked.

"For actual money?" I asked. "No chance." Orion and I gave them away to build goodwill with our audience when we were busking.

Just then, Mom said, "Okay, close your eyes. Here comes our first Portland bridge."

I squeezed my eyes shut. Mom made a little money by helping with bridge tours, and she got to see all kinds of cool things close-up. Ships and boats and fish and peregrine falcons and a sea lion that bobbed up by a Willamette River dock. I could even chant the bridge names. Morrison. Fremont. Broadway. St. Johns. Burnside. Marquam. Hawthorne. Ross Island. Sellwood. Steel. Just the way she did it when she was telling us the story of seeing stars in the water that told her what Orion's name should be. "Now!" Mom said.

We were in the middle of a bridge over the wide Willamette River. I caught a glimpse of a ship.

"I've never seen the new bridge," Mom said. "Tilikum Crossing. No cars allowed, so maybe it's gotten to be people's favorite."

My favorite bridge would be the one that carried us out of here, running like the river runs. As soon as we were on the other side, I saw two glass fingers pointed to the sky. Maybe five minutes later, Mom steered us expertly off I-5, and soon we drove by a coffee shop and into in a neighborhood of small, scruffy houses where streetlights were coming on.

No splashy views here. No dunes or wildflowers or whales. No Mount Hood, even—it had completely disappeared. You could live your whole life in this neighborhood and not even know the big mountain existed right outside your city.

At an oak tree with moss crawling up its sides, Mom turned. Yellow, green, and blue bins lined the street. "There's free money in those," I told Edom.

"Really?" Edom leaned forward eagerly.

Mom rolled her window down and called to a guy with silver-gray hair who was lugging a yellow bin to the curb. "Anything I should know about parking?"

He gave her a wide smile. "Around here, you can cheerfully park any old thing any old where." He set the tub down. Bottles clinked.

Orion and I would have raced each other to check out those bottles. Now I'd have to be the one to teach Edom how people were mostly too busy to take their bottles and cans to redemption centers.

Mom had barely gotten the cello unbuckled before the guy came across the street. "Welcome to Portland," he said. "The place where we can let our freak flags fly in the middle of the street. I'm Victor, by the way."

The main interesting thing about Victor was the blue scrunchie holding his hair back. Also, he had blue eyes like Dad and like me.

Mom introduced all of us and said to Edom, "A nice

neighbor, see? We'll write to Amy and tell her you have a warm and safe place to stay, just like she wanted."

"You bet," Victor said.

The opposite of what I wanted.

Mom handed out the pillowcases from the trunk and led us in a parade past a yard that was weedier than a Rainbow Farm pasture. Seriously, whoever lived there should get a goat. Also, people around here must think moss was an excellent plant. No exaggeration.

A teenager with purple-streaked hair and a tank top swerved down the street on a skateboard, steered onto the sidewalk and popped her board up and under her arm.

Bam!

"Ollie nollie kickflip," Orion and I said constantly when I was in third grade and he was teaching me to ride. The most interesting thing about the teenager—besides her skateboard—was a butterfly tattoo. I saw wings spread over her shoulders, and antennas tickling her neck.

"That would be Jessica," said Victor as the girl turned into the weedy yard.

Jessica? Was that name stuck to me now no matter where I went?

"Defender of grandmothers and bees," Victor added.

I didn't point out that bees could defend themselves perfectly well with their stingers. Instead, I stared after her, wondering how long it would be before she let me ride that skateboard. Finally, I ran up the steps, across the shabby porch, and into the little house where Mom had led the others.

Bare walls, bare floors. A frizz of new smells. Empty bedroom to the left—where Mom was putting her things down—and empty living room to the right. From the living room I could see a second bedroom and the kitchen. Nothing more.

I'd only shared a sleeping place with family members, which, technically, Edom was, but I hadn't gotten used to that idea yet.

Awkward.

Well, maybe she'd insist on sharing a room with Mom.

All of us—including Victor—sat in a circle on the bare floor and ate cake from Madam Marie's basket, which wasn't the greatest supper in the world, but it was something. Through a bare window, I saw an airplane lift up and up. "Let's finish while daylight is still on our side," Mom said, brushing crumbs off Edom's face. "Edom, you go with Jupiter." She turned to Victor. "Want to help?"

Mom knew how to make friends fast. We all did. That was the way with buskers.

Edom followed me, frowning and silent, as I showed her the routine Orion had made up. Put the flashlight in a place where you can find it easily when you wake up in a dark, strange room. Unroll your sleeping bag. Fluff your squashed pillow. Brush your teeth—luckily, water ran out of the faucet.

After Edom was in her sleeping bag, I went out to help with the last load.

"Thanks, Victor," Mom said when she saw me. "We can take it from here."

"Bye, Victor!" I shouted after him.

When we were back inside, Mom locked the door behind us. "We'll return the car and get utilities switched over to my name tomorrow," she said.

Utilities was a bad word in our family. "Do you have enough money?" I asked.

Mom's face looked yellow in the streetlight coming through the window. "Orion got an advance from the café."

Orion slaving away so we could have light from switches and little flames on our stove? Mom and I had to get our busk on *immediately*.

Mom must have been thinking the same thing because she said, "We'll start making money soon." She opened the MISCELLANEOUS box. "What do you think for Edom? Tambourine?"

A tambourine and a cute kid would be a definite crowd pleaser. But people staring at Edom? No way.

Even after I went to bed, I kept thinking about utilities. I was an expert at taking a bath in two inches of water and roasting a marshmallow over a candle. Once, we had stayed in a mountain cabin down a gravel road, while Mom and Topher repaired the deck that hung out over a creek. Orion and I had lugged icy-cold buckets of water into the house. Every time I washed, I could hear Dad in my head saying, "That water'll toughen you up." He'd always helped me be tough.

Edom flopped over with a little moan. It seemed like all night she was thrashing around, and when I opened my eyes the next morning, her sleeping bag was empty, which scared me, even though there was only that one time on the road that something seriously bad had happened.

Chapter Ten

A-begging buttermilk I will go,
But I won't be a beggar long,
I know an old woman at yonder farm
Who will give me plenty if I ask for some.
I'll sell it all for one penny,
Fol the lol the laddle dee,
And with that penny I will buy eggs,
And I shall have seven for my penny.

I poked my head out the bedroom door. The living room was empty and the front door was open a crack.

Uh-oh.

Technically, I wasn't in charge of Edom. No one had even asked me if I wanted Edom to be part of our family. She could go all the way back to Ethiopia and it wouldn't, technically, be my responsibility.

But she didn't know how alert you should be, like one morning when I was heading sleepily outside and suddenly saw a bobcat preparing to walk right up the steps of Paddy Wagon.

No scary stories, Jupiter.

Dad said if you tell yourself a story about this or that danger, or how you need something to be happy, or how you're going to be unbearably cold and hungry or wet unless you store up money and stuff, you're trapped.

I crept across the living room all full of weird dread. The planet Jupiter is so strong that stars and moons around it wobble. But now I had a little moon in my gravitational field that was making *me* wobble.

I checked Mom's room. She was snoring softly. She had the superpower of sleep.

Quick. Quick. My feet made soft sounds against the wood floor.

I swung the front door open.

Edom was sitting on the steps wearing her nightgown with sandals. She had a white shawl wrapped around her shoulder. A couple of crows in the street squawked at me. "You shouldn't be out here alone," I said.

"Why not? I can use my noodle." She nudged something beside her that clinked.

A bottle. In fact, nine of them lined up. "Where did you get the loot?"

"She showed me." Edom pointed and I saw the teenager from next door standing on the sidewalk with one foot on her skateboard. A sign under her arm said BRING BACK THE POLLINATORS. I wanted to call out and tell her I'd read that *National Geographic* article a hundred times. *They are the Earth's pollinators. And they come in more than 200,000 shapes and sizes.*

"Hi," I called instead. My voice sounded weirdly loud in the mizzly air.

Jessica saluted me and tick-tacked off. "Do you know how early it is?" I asked Edom.

"I don't have a watch."

"Well," I said. "Next time wait until I get up. And aren't you cold?"

Edom only said, "I was going to take *all* the bottles. She said some were no good."

I showed her how to check the label to be sure it said OR 5¢ refund value. "We can get five cents for each of these," I explained. "Did you look in the blue bin?"

"There's easy money in the blue bins, too?" Edom brightened.

"Sometimes. Like aluminum cans. Let's get dressed and I'll show you."

It didn't take long for us to pull on clothes and shoes and sweaters—and for me to grab the jar of blessed thistle, which I left on the front porch. Across the street, I tipped Victor's blue bin so Edom could lift the lid and stick her head in. "I see a bunch of paper." Her voice echoed. I laid the bin flat and she crawled inside. "I see one aluminum can."

I checked it to be sure. Yep. Aluminum. "If I can find a wagon to pull, we can load up next week," I told her as we walked back to our own porch. "We'll beat everyone else to the good stuff." I opened the jar of blessed thistle and started sprinkling it.

"What's that?" Edom asked.

"Nothing." No need to bring up Topher. Maybe he'd had time to amaze her with his mad tightrope-walking skills. When they were on the trip, did he sing her to sleep? Did he teach her how to make a drum out of anything? "One time," I told Edom, "Orion and I collected so much aluminum and glass money that we bought everyone new sleeping bags."

"How many places have you lived?" She was on the top step with her chin in her hands.

"Technically, too many to count."

"Did anything bad ever happen?"

Only that one time, and I wasn't going to talk about it. I didn't even want to think about it. I gave her a good look. "Hey, I didn't know you wore glasses."

"I found them in my bag. Amy-mom got them for me in Ethiopia."

Maybe that was some of the rustling I'd heard in the night. "How many places have you lived?" I screwed the lid back on the jar. "And did you live in a house, or what?"

She straightened. The glasses made her eyes owly. "You think I lived in a hut, don't you? You think I ran around with giraffes."

"No!" I said. "I already know you lived in a city."

"My grandma doesn't," she said. "She doesn't have electricity."

I waited, but she didn't say anything more, so I

studied the lay of the land. My stomach growled. "Hey, I've got a good idea," I said. "Your recycling can help pay for our lunch."

"I found the bottles." She held out the aluminum can. "You can share this one with me."

Wow. Seriously? It wasn't the little bit of money but the principle. "Don't you care about helping the family?" I gave her my most charming smile. "Won't it feel good to do something sweet for Mom?" I didn't even say "and me."

"No." She put the can down on the porch.

"But—"

"I don't care," she said, not letting me finish. "I'm going to keep the money."

Wow. I'd never before met someone who was like mean John McCann in real life.

Chapter Eleven

The boss's name was John McCann
You know, he was a blamed mean man
Last week a premature blast went off
And a mile in the air went big Jim Goff.
And when next payday came around
Jim Goff a dollar short was found
When he asked, "What for?" came this reply
"You were docked for the time you were up in the sky."

My stomach felt as hollow as a guitar's belly. I thought about the coffee shop blocks away and imagined I could smell cinnamon and fresh baked goods all the way from there to here. I was that hungry.

Why was I on this porch when I could be hanging out at the coast with Orion watching jellyfish, which according to *National Geographic*, have lasted for 650 million years even with no brains, no heart, and no blood? Instead, I was stuck with someone who put her fellow human beings behind the almighty buck.

My family shared whatever anyone made from busking tips or jobs. Dad used to sing about the railroad driller, Jim Goff, who was blasted up in the air, and how John McCann docked the driller's pay for the time he was up in the sky. At the end, Dad would say, "That's what some folks do. Put their fellow man behind the almighty buck."

"Jupiter?" It was Mom calling from inside. "Edom?"

"Tell Mom I'll be back," I said to Edom. "She knows I have the superpower of not getting lost."

"Can I come?" Edom called as I ran down the sidewalk.

"No," I shouted back. I wasn't mad. But I sure was irked.

Crows were cawing furiously at a cat that trotted along the street. A young woman pushing a stroller jogged by and waved as I checked the yellow bins. One house had twinkle lights. One yard had an old stove turned into a planter. I took a bag from a recycling bin to carry my loot in.

Then I started to sing—bitterly, at first.

"I'm a one-way train,

Rattling down the track.

You can come along, along.

But I'm not coming back."

I was chilly and hungry. Right this second, Orion was probably flipping eggs. Dad was on a beach somewhere singing to the sizzle of a breakfast *iguana*. Aunt Amy was eating in her bed and waiting to hear from Edom. Topher . . . who cared what Topher was doing?

Ahead was the Heart of Wisdom Zen Temple. JOIN US IN THE PRACTICE OF SILENT LOVING KINDNESS said a sign in the window. A few doors down, a woman was on her porch drinking coffee. I picked up three soggy, rolled-up newspapers from the sidewalk and juggled them—*thwack, thwack*. Starring . . . Jupiter! She clapped. I bowed, and she held out a plate of muffins.

So there was breakfast, no problem. I hesitated over one with cranberries poking out versus one with oat topping. "Take both," she said, so I did. I said thank you, and walked on, munching happily.

Planet Jupiter has an extremely strong magnetic field.

Last month, the principal of my school came into the lunchroom every day and gave a ticket to anyone who was eating quietly. At the end of lunch, she pulled the number of one ticket. You didn't even get a prize except having the whole lunchroom turn and look at special you.

That's what busking was like.

People thought buskers were fascinating—except every once in a while when they hassled you.

Up the block, a girl was checking the yellow bins and calling in Spanish to the driver of a car. The competition. Well, it was time to quit anyway. "Don't sit up there and cry!" I shouted to a seagull on a roof. "Head to the ocean!"

When I got back, Mom was putting a pot pathetically all by itself on a kitchen shelf. She was born to play music, not keep house. "Where's Edom?" I asked, opening the bag to show her.

"Exploring the backyard." Mom's hair glinted as she nodded toward the window. She and Madam Marie had done the hair colors as an experiment, giggling together.

I walked to the window. The backyard looked scruffy, and a blackberry cane was reaching over the wall from Jessica's backyard. In the corner between the two yards was a tree with branches that drooped to the ground.

Edom was peering under the tree branches. Deciding where to bury her treasure? I wanted to tell Mom that Edom said she didn't care about us, but I didn't want to hurt Mom's feelings. And what if Mom took Edom's side?

Serious tough beans for me!

Chapter Twelve

When I die take my saddle from the wall
Put it on my pony, lead him out of his stall
Tie my bones to his back, turn our faces to the west
And we'll ride the prairies that we love the best

I told Mom about the muffins and that I didn't need anything from the basket. Mom ate breakfast leaning against the kitchen counter, and Edom ate leaning against Mom. "All right, curly girl," Mom said. "Time to try what you told me Amy-mom does." I watched her start taking Edom's hair out of braids, combing it with her fingers.

It made me wish I were still little enough for her to do my hair.

I got out an envelope and made a big deal of writing

"Food Money" on it. Then I found the hammer and nails in a box and hung my beads on my bedroom wall.

After we were in the car, Mom explained our first stop: the Community Warehouse, where Victor said we could get beds. Customers usually went through an agency to apply, but we were skipping that step. Who wouldn't melt to hear Edom's sad story?

We pulled into the parking lot, where a sign said TO HAVE A PLACE TO SIT AND THINK, YOU NEED A PLACE TO SIT. Mom told me to take Edom to the book section. Away from staring eyes. Edom found a book of fairy tales. I read one on edible wild plants until I got to the part on look-alike plants. You chewed them up and swallowed and *then* found out they could cause death.

Seriously?

"Success!" Mom said coming up to us. "Three beds—delivered tomorrow."

On the way home, we spotted a free couch. Victor walked back with us and helped lug it into our living room. He also gave us eggs from his chickens.

See? I wanted to tell Orion. We were managing fine.

That afternoon, as we set off again, I was half

listening to Mom go through our plans—buy groceries, go to the library, where Mom could use a computer to get utilities set up, go downtown to return the rental car, come back home on the city bus. Mostly though, I was thinking about money.

We'd always spent a chunk of whatever money we made to buy gas for the Paddy Wagon. Food could cost a lot, so we filled in with soup kitchens and food banks and gleaning. If we wanted to stay in a cabin or yurt, we might have to pay, although lots of times people would trade for repairs. Laundromats were strictly cash. Usually coins.

Usually we were fine without money.

I wished I could explain to Edom that people think if they buy this or that thing, they'll be happy forever. It doesn't take long before they're right back to however much happiness they started with.

Mom pulled into the Safeway lot. "Let's redeem your bottles," she said. "Then we'll find something for our supper that doesn't have to be refrigerated."

"Something light," I said. "Because we have to carry it home on the bus."

"Something not smelly," Edom said. "Because you said we're going to the library."

What did she think Mom was going to buy?

A man with a stocking cap let us go ahead of him and even helped us feed our bottles into the clinking-clanking machine and get the credit slips out. I made a big deal of showing Edom I was handing mine over to Mom.

In Safeway, we picked out a small bag of granola, a quart of milk, rice, and dried beans. "What kind of fruit?" Mom asked.

"Oranges!" I said. I hadn't had even *one* the whole time we lived at Rainbow Farm. My inner eye saw the skin peeling back and drops of juice exploding toward my tongue.

But Mom reached for a carton of strawberries. "From California," she said, pointing to the sign. "Amy might be eating some right now." She and Edom smiled at each other.

I had a bit of luck, though, when we were on our way to the library and ended up on a street lined with small shops. "Stop," I called out. "I think I saw a wagon in that thrift store."

Mom handed back ten bucks—no questions—because a wagon was always a good investment. "You hop out, too," she told Edom. "Maybe you'll find something you need. Keep a good eye on her," she added to me.

After a long minute, Edom gave in and undid her seat belt.

Just bashy! Jupiter and her moon. "Stick close," I told Edom as we walked toward the store. Busking had given me plenty of skills for handling anyone who acted like a scuzzbag. I caught sight of a sign for an Ethiopian restaurant a few blocks away, but I didn't say anything because Edom wasn't even trying—and Mom? Of course I wanted Mom to be nice to Edom, but I was her daughter. She should be even nicer to me.

It didn't take me long to pick out three sparkly bean bags—for juggling—and ask if the clerk would throw them in with the wagon and also hold the wagon until I could pick it up. As I was paying, Edom slid a beat-up old doll onto the counter. "Why would you want that?" I asked. "Spend more of your money and get one that isn't shabby."

She shook her head. I shrugged and bargained the woman down. "It can be a lookout for Mom," I told Edom, setting it on the windowsill at the front of the store. She snatched it up. I pulled my ponytail across my face and pretended it was a mustache, but Edom only looked out the window longingly until we spotted the car.

"Utilities all set!" Mom said as we got in. "And another stroke of luck I'll tell you about when I'm not concentrating on driving. Help me watch for the Union Station tower that says 'Go by train.' The rental car place is close to the train and bus stations."

As we drove off, I could feel the city squeezing all around me. I would go by train or any other way at all, if I could only go.

Chapter Thirteen

Well, I look upon the mountain.
Tip my face up to the sun.
I must leave my home tomorrow
Running as the river runs.
Do not tell them that I'm leaving.
They will miss me when I'm gone.
But though it breaks my heart to go
I must be rambling on.

The most interesting thing about the Broadway Bridge, according to Mom, was that it could open up if a ship had to pass through. We drove out over the water. "There!" I shouted. "'Go by Train!'"

"You can buy a train?" Edom asked.

Mom was still explaining about *by* and *buy* when I spotted the rental car place.

The woman who checked us in told us where to catch the TriMet city bus back home. "Stay alert," she said. "People get confused by the one-way streets here all the time."

Right away, we did get a little confused and a lot distracted!

First there was the skateboard store ("Skaters serving skaters since 1976") with its cool window displays. Then Mom wanted to walk by sculpted lilies—red, yellow, green, and blue glass—towering over the sidewalk. When I reached to touch one, a voice called, "Look out."

I jumped back.

A skateboarder with a guitar on her back bumped past. "It's carnivorous," she said.

Wow. A lily that size could swallow a kid no problem.

"In real life, I mean," she shouted over her shoulder as she turned the corner. "Not the sculpture."

Oh. I knew that.

Mom stopped to study a TriMet bus sign, and a young black guy peddled past and called, "Keep a good eye on those kids around here."

Edom grabbed Mom's hand. I felt like grabbing the other hand but I kept my dignity.

I spotted the back of the Greyhound station, then a woman sleeping in a doorway, and then . . .

"Look!" Mom pointed across the street. "I volunteered at that Sisters of the Road Café almost twenty years ago!"

The ground in front of the café was covered with people and bags. A man with a black beard came weaving toward us, but when I gave him the stink eye, he respected my personal space. Edom shrank against Mom. "Left at the corner," I told them. "I'm sure."

When we finally found the bus stop, Edom sat on the bench glued to Mom, looking slightly desperate. Mom showed her an oil puddle. "Rainbows," she said.

I thought of Orion steering me around a broken bottle, asking, "Remember when we saw that field of glass, and Mom told us it was fairy wings? *Glass?* What if we had picked it up?"

But we hadn't, had we?

The bus pulled up. Mom gave us each a dollar twenty-five and we followed her up the steps, paid our fares, and settled into a seat.

So what if Mom saw fairy wings in glass and

rainbows in puddles? She had imagination. When I complained about free-lunch food, she and I dreamed up ideal lunches. Apricots and asparagus and abalone. Cheese and cherries. I suggested chocolate. Madam Marie suggested chard. Mom suggested chili in a thermos and sent some with me in real life the next mizzly day.

Now I leaned against her, wishing we had some of that chili for supper.

The best thing on this bus was a black dog with a harness that said, "Guide for the blind." The dog's owner looked a little like Edom. The red-headed woman beside him kept reporting where we were. Greyhound Bus Station. Steel Bridge. An event center with huge painted basketball players. So many city buildings that I could almost feel myself being squeezed smaller. At the next stop, a young woman wearing a pink helmet rolled up the ramp in her wheelchair. The bus driver came back to fold up bus seats. "Seem snug?" she asked, securing the chair.

"As a rug," the woman said.

Snug rugs were fine . . . if you were a bug, or Edom. I sighed. "What was the stroke of luck at the library?" I asked.

Mom played air guitar. "A gig. At a farmers' market."

We were going to be fine! Of course we were.

"I did a quick search for child-busking laws," Mom said. "Didn't find anything except if Portland police want to hassle a busker, they have to wait until the song is done."

I'd had plenty of practice looking over my shoulder but that didn't mean I liked it.

When we got home, I trotted across the street to where Victor was studying a skinny tree hung with a sign that said FRIENDS OF TREES. "Know anything about cops and busking in Portland?" I asked.

"I've got a friend who busks with his typewriter and creates poems on demand," Victor said. "He says it's always a hustle and don't quit your day job."

Too negative. I changed the subject. "It's a baby tree, huh? Are those your chickens making that racket?"

"Sure is and sure are." He grinned at me. "I can smell rain in the air, but I think it's going north. June in Portland is such a tease. And come July, the rain will dry up like someone turned off a spigot."

That couldn't be right. I remembered June at the

coast and racing down a sidewalk with rain pelting us, past umbrellas turning inside out. All I said, though, was, "If you save all your redeemable bottles for me, I'll come collect them and you won't have to lug them to the curb."

He nodded. "You need money, huh? It doesn't add up too fast, five cents at a time."

"Got a better suggestion?"

"You could find gems in the sagebrush hills of eastern Oregon. Jaspers. Agates. Opals."

"How far away?"

"Seven-and-a-half, eight hours. Oregon is a rock hound's dream." He adjusted his scrunchie. "If you can't find gemstones in the Owyhee Mountains, better get another hobby."

I'd consider it. No idea was too goofy for getting Orion back.

Chapter Fourteen

One of these days, and it won't be long
Call my name and I'll be gone.
Fare-thee-well, O Honey, fare-thee-well.

One thing I'd learned from camping in isolated places like Cape Blanco State Park and Imperial Sand Dunes was that opportunity can knock when you least expect it. The next day, after our beds were delivered, I sat on mine and spread out Dad's postcards.

Dad had some weird way of always knowing where we were. Blind mole-rat vibrations. Or Mom was secretly in touch with him, even though she claimed she wasn't.

Each postcard had pretty much the same message. Infinite possibilities.

For the next week and a half, I got the lay of the land. Sometimes Edom wanted to tag along, but I always told her no. A little moss on Planet Jupiter could do a lot to mess things up.

Victor helped me retrieve the wagon. The Saturday morning of the gig, he took me with him to trade chicken eggs for a neighbor's duck eggs. "How's settling in?" he called to Mom, who was pulling some cute pants for Edom out of a bag she got at a free clothing exchange.

"Great," Mom said. She'd been working hard on odd jobs around the neighborhood.

I hadn't told her how Edom never seemed to sleep at night.

For seven blocks or so, people kept saying "Hey, Victor." A guy with a carved walking stick said, "What's up, old man?"

"We codgers got to stick together," Victor said tapping the stick. He seemed to know everyone around here.

When we were done and circling back, Victor

pointed out a restaurant that had kale growing in the yard. "Popular with locavores," he said. He swung the basket lightly. "You know what a carnivore is?"

"Meat-eater," I said. Like . . . lilies.

"Herbivore?"

"Eats plants."

"A locavore eats things grown locally." He gave a thumbs-up to a young man jingling a set of keys. "Hey, Prop. What's baking today?

"Pea-blossom-and-garlic wood-fired pizza. Come try it sometime," he told me. "This old guy, he's a skeptic, but I can tell you're a Portland hipster."

"I think his name's short for *Propaganda,*" Victor said. "He's always got some convincing going on."

"I'm a busker," I told Prop. "So let me know any time the restaurant would like some entertainment." As we walked on, I could feel my mojo popping.

When you busked, anything could happen. A tourist might speak to you in Japanese. Or toss pesos or rubles or shillings in the lucky hat. One time someone dropped in ointment for a skateboarding scrape on my leg. But another time, someone set off a firecracker so close that

Orion and I practically jumped out of our skeletons.

We crossed an intersection where painted fish gulped along the street. Victor gave me the whole basket of duck eggs. "They have more omega three and more protein than my chicken eggs," he said. "I'll be back for all of you and that cello."

I ran up the steps, checking the mail slot. Edom had already gotten lots of letters from Aunt Amy. I hadn't gotten a single postcard yet.

Inside, Mom was hanging a piece of fabric to warm up the bare living room. "Don't overcook the eggs," I said. "The duck person said they'll get rubbery."

Mom looked flushed and distracted the way we all got on busking days. I grabbed some bread and cheese, put out my Mardi Gras beads, packed origami birds in our lucky velvet bag, and drank a glass of warm water. Presenting . . . the amazing Jupiter! By tonight, I might have farmers' market dark honey for my vocal cords. We could even be famous, like the Portland street musician who had gotten almost to the finals on *The Voice*.

There were famous sister singers like the Dixie Chicks, and Lennon and Maisy, but except for the Judds,

I couldn't think of any other mother-daughters.

When we were discovered, what then?

The fame would be good enough for me . . . and knowing people were listening to our music. I wouldn't want to get off the road. Maybe for a while, though, Mom and I could settle in a tiny house on a wild part of the coast near a college—for Orion. With a dog. Dad could visit. And we could buy oranges whenever we wanted.

Mom interrupted my daydream. "Victor's here to drive us. Will you get Edom, please," she called. "She's got some kind of project going in the backyard."

I trotted out and down the back steps, sticking out my tongue and counting loudly to help relax my jaw. That's when I saw that Edom's project involved my wagon.

She jumped up and tried to block my view. "Your mom said I could use it."

Technically, Mom couldn't give permission for Edom to use *my* wagon. Behind her arms, I caught sight of little pots and plants with maroon leaves and small yellow flowers.

"Where did you get the loot?" I asked.

Edom squeezed her mouth until her lips disappeared, but she gave herself away with her eyes. I followed her glance and headed for the tree in the corner. When I crawled under the droopy branches to peer into our neighbor's back yard, I saw an even huger mess of weeds than the front yard. Also, a shed. With the door open.

Ha! Edom was a thief!

Some people thought all buskers were thieves. But we'd never stolen anything.

I crawled back out and all I said was, "Time to go." Let Edom sweat for now. I would tell when I was ready. For now, I wasn't going to spoil our first busking gig. But Mom was definitely going to be upset when she found out about this.

Chapter Fifteen

I don't like Old Joe Clark,
Don't think I ever shall.
I don't like Old Joe Clark,
Always liked his girl.

"Cute," Victor said, winking at me as he helped Edom load the wagon into the back of his car. She had made a sign that said $1.00 EACH.

Not cute. I sat in the car blowing soft raspberries into my hands to get my singing lips relaxed. As we drove, Mom and Victor talked about famous Portland buskers. Hula hoopers. A bucket drummer. The Unipiper, a unicyclist who wore a Darth Vader mask while playing flaming bagpipes.

Mom and I had a little kid, which always warms a crowd up because they want her to succeed. Too bad this one hated being stared at.

It took only about five minutes before I spotted the booths of a farmers' market in a huge school parking lot.

Busking time!

As we parked, Mom turned around to face me. "I'd like you to help Edom with her project today," she said.

"What?" I said. "Seriously?"

Victor steered Edom out of the car and around to the back, while Mom leaned her arm on the seat to get closer to me. "See how hard she's trying to help?"

Wrong! Edom probably wasn't planning to even *share* any money she made. Besides . . . "Mom," I said, "you need me to sing!"

"It's okay. It's only an hour slot. I'll be fine on my own."

Not okay! I huffed out of the car, longing for Orion.

"Jupiter is very resourceful," Mom told Victor as we walked past houses and toward the farmers' market sign of an umbrella (of course) with a rooster perched on it. "You want her on your side when you're planning your busk."

I'd better be resourceful because Edom wasn't a registered vendor.

The farmers' market turned out to have about thirty-five booths. Nothing big and fancy like the four-block-long one we often worked in California. Mom got ready, rubbing her right arm and elbow the way she did when it hurt from playing too many Irish jigs or spending too much time with a caulking gun. Poor Mom. And she wasn't even letting me help.

Did busking mojo go away if it got rusty? If the busking poet broke his arm, would his rhymes and rhythms get frozen inside of him?

It was a scary thought.

I set the lucky money basket in front of Mom's chair, added a dollar to prime the pump, and took a handful of origami birds out of the lucky velvet bag. I gave a bird to everyone who walked by. "Hello," I said. "That's my mom on the cello. You have a good day."

Most people smiled back. One hello, one small victory for humankind.

Then I found Edom a spot under a tree on the park side of the market, still in sight of Mom and close to good booths, but not obvious enough to draw attention of any official. At least that's what I hoped.

Edom didn't complain as she unloaded all her pots and propped up her sign and sat down with the shabby doll in her lap.

By now, Mom was deep into a jaunty song, "Who Will Buy this Wonderful Morning?" Upbeat. To put customers in a good mood.

"Good luck," I told Edom. Then I headed to the Beary Berry Honey booth. The vendor might give me some honey if I offered to watch things while she took a break at a way different kind of honey place—the Honey Bucket port-a-potty. Also, I wanted to see if I could spot any farmers' market officials doing inspections.

I glanced back. Edom was sitting completely still on her blanket. No one was approaching her, because she wasn't making eye contact.

Well, tough beans.

I had scoped things out pretty well and was reaching for a sample of pear chutney, when behind me I heard a woman's voice say, "Where's your mother? I need a word with her."

Uh-oh.

I raced over to the Green Eggs and Ham booth to see better. A woman in a short green dress, leggings, and Birkenstocks was standing over Edom.

Dogs and strollers and people were starting to knot into a little crowd. The woman was like the giant Pacific octopus at the Newport aquarium. Really sure of herself. The kind of thing that's hard to look away from.

I started weaving through the shoppers.

Edom deserved to be munched. But I saw her face all crumply, and remembered an old-timey song Topher used to sing, "Orphan children sees a hard time in this world."

"Hello, ma'am," I said, stepping in front of Edom, who took the chance to scramble backward. "I hope you're having a nice day."

"Did the farmers' market really approve selling this nuisance plant?" The woman put her hands on her hips. "That's hard to believe, considering it's got a deep, tough root that saps water from other plants. Once it gets established, it's impossible to get rid of."

So Edom didn't steal the plants? They were weeds? "Yes," I said. "Well . . ."

"Who's the adult in charge here?" She looked around. Her next step would be to find an official and bring us down.

Suddenly, I heard a girl say, "That's oxalis. Food you don't even have to plant."

The woman and I both turned. The girl was maybe fourteen and wore a fluffy black skirt and a pink top with sequins and beads. Pretty fancy.

"You're friends of weeds, huh?" The girl smiled at me and Edom. "So are we." A taller girl stepped up beside her, pausing to take a selfie. She had on jeans and a T-shirt that said "Love a Weed—Eat Local." She turned her phone to take a picture of Edom's wagon.

My competitive instincts kicked in. "Hey," I said. "That's private property."

"We're the Foodie Twins," the fancy girl told the octopus woman.

Twins? They didn't look like twins.

"With this plant," the woman said, "one year's

seeding makes seven years' weeding."

Edom squirmed like a little prey fish trying to blend in to its environment.

"There are about 850 species of oxalis." The fancy girl waved her phone to say she'd looked it up. "Don't plant this in your garden plot, but keep it safely in a pot."

Wow. What was their gig?

She turned toward the shoppers. "In fact, we're putting together a block-walk to show off this plant and others," she said. "Here's some information."

It was one thing to help us out, but what made these so-called twins think they could take over? My back started going all prickly, like I was a cat defending its territory. No exaggeration.

Chapter Sixteen

I put my hand in a rosy bush
Thinking the sweetest flower to find.
I stabbed my finger to the bone,
And left the sweetest flower behind.

It was an unspoken rule of buskers not to crowd each other's spots. Apparently these two hadn't gotten the memo.

"A farmers' market is *made* for kids," the tall girl said. People paused and smiled. The octopus took the chance to fade back into the crowd, and Edom scurried off to Mom.

"I'm Danielle," she continued.

"And I'm Moria," the fancy girl said. "We have a web page and podcasts and—"

"I got this spot first," I said.

Danielle acted like she didn't hear me. "We fell in love with good, healthy food at a farmers' market," she said to the group.

"You're not really twins," I said, interrupting.

Moria turned. "You don't know how many people have said that. When we were in third grade, our classmates didn't believe it, even though we had the same last name and were dropped off by the same person."

Danielle took up the story. "Finally we said, 'Ask us our dog's name.' I went out on the playground and Moria stayed in the classroom. I said, 'My dog is named Yoshi.'"

"And *I* said, 'My dog is named Yoshi.'" Moria took a small bow.

People laughed. "Clever," a guy called.

I wanted to be clever.

"Who tried something yummy today?" Danielle asked.

"I tried pear chutney," I said. Well, almost. A few people applauded. That was a sound I always wanted more, more, more of.

"Exceptional answer!" Danielle started blabbing about how to get kids to try new food. Seriously?

I had a memory of Dad lifting me out of the sea and tossing me high in the salty sunshine. "What an exceptional girl!" he was saying. When I got older, he explained about my mojo.

First, he said, I was one cool cucumber.

Second, I could talk to anyone.

Third, I could sing. "With all that going for you," he said, "you'll always be able to take care of yourself and do big things in the world."

I never got out-mojoed by other kids. But it was hard to get more exceptional than *twins*.

Now Danielle was scooping up one of Edom's pots. "If you're careful and do your research, you can even eat weeds. These colorful little leaves are refreshing to nibble on. Add the tiny yellow flowers to salads or make them into something tart to drink. See?" She passed her phone around.

I gave the screen a good look. Topher had fed us something like this at the cabin—same leaf shape, different color.

Time for some self-respect. I grabbed the pot back, picked a friendly face, and made eye contact. "Sir, you look brave enough to go first," I said. "Would you try it?"

He stepped toward me. Mom's cello was crescendoing in the background, synching everyone's heartbeat in a feel-good moment, at least according to what Mom always said about music.

I held my breath. The guy pinched a leaf and put it on his tongue. "Not bad," he said, chewing. More people paused to see what was going on.

"Goes beautifully with pear chutney," I told him. He laughed, like I'd hoped he would. Laughter always makes people want to come in closer. "If you're a locavore," I called out, "you can't get any more local than this."

"No worries about oxalis leaching calcium out of your bones," Danielle chimed in. "You would have to munch on it night and day for months like a force-fed lab rat."

I tried to think of a clever retort about lab rats.

"Want to know what else has oxalic acid?" Moria consulted her phone. "Tea, parsley, rhubarb, spinach, cocoa, chocolate, nuts, berries, black pepper, and beans."

"But try a bit first to make sure you're not allergic." Danielle started handing out flyers. "We'll teach you all about oxalis and other edibles on our block-walk. And if you have kids with you today, we'll have a demonstration for them right over there, in the park."

The park? They better not poach my crowd. *Speak up. Stand tall.* "Will you all take one step forward?" I said.

Pack mentality. It almost always wins. "Care to get us started?" I asked the man with the friendly face. "A girl has to make a living."

That line usually worked for Orion and me. Sure enough. The man fished out his dollar.

I took it with a flourish and a bow. "Remember. Don't put this plant in your garden plot," I said. "Keep it cozy in a pot." If one of the so-called twins protested I was stealing their slogan, I'd say what I'd heard another busker say: "Hey, man, I don't see any copyright symbol here."

Anyway, I'd made their slogan better.

With Mom's cello music beneath my wings, I chatted and made change and sold those plants as fast as I could. A woman took the last two plants, handed me a five-dollar bill, and said, "Keep the change."

"Thank you," Danielle said, as if the woman were talking to her. "If you try oxalis and you like the taste, consider coming on our block-walk week after next."

Week after next, she and Moria better find their own spot to hustle from.

I headed for Mom. Edom was sitting in the cello's shadow, and I made a big show of giving Mom the velvet bag stuffed with bills. If she paid attention, she'd see how Edom refused to share the money even though *I* made it for her.

Edom didn't look stubborn anymore, sitting there hugging the doll. "When that woman yelled at me," she said, "my heart started going bounce bounce bounce."

"You remind me of Serena, the collie pup at Rainbow Farm," I told her. "It didn't want us around at first. It even tried to bite Orion and me."

"If it didn't want you around, why didn't you leave it alone?" Edom asked.

"I don't know," I said. Well, I did know, but I didn't want to say.

Zeb had shaken his head when he first saw it. "All scarified. Afeared. Skeert. What are you gonna do?" But Edom was worse—like sticking my hand in a rosy bush and getting big-time stabbed by a thorn.

Chapter Seventeen

Every night when the sun goes in.
Every night when the sun goes in.
Every night when the sun goes in,
I hang my head and mournful cry.

What *was* I gonna do?

I wasn't going to hang my head and mournful cry—
that was for sure. I was going to prove where she got
the pots, and then Mom would know the trouble I'd
seen.

As Victor drove us home, Mom was bubbly and
triumphant. Someone had told her about the Portland
Cello Project, a horde of anywhere from eight to sixteen
cellos dedicated to bringing the cello to places you

wouldn't normally hear it. A guy who put in a ten-dollar bill told her he was addicted to two Croatian cellists whose YouTube video has gotten millions of hits. "I got to reserve another spot," she said. "In two weeks."

"When those girls show up again I'll be ready," I said. I made a fierce face to show how I would stand my ground and command my space.

"Your new friends?" Mom asked. "They looked helpful."

Friends? Try *the competition.* "By the way, if you want to sell things," I said to Edom, "you have to engage people. Next week, that shabby doll has got to go. It's pathetic."

Edom chewed on the sleeve of her sweater. Some people have expressions written on their face with a thin pencil. When you're trying to build a crowd, you don't focus on a face like Edom's, all private.

When Victor parked, Edom ran ahead of me up the steps and to the mail basket. Another yellow envelope? Then I saw what else she was holding.

A postcard. Finally!

On the front, a bear was standing tall, looking like

the king of the mountain. On the back, Dad had written, "Around here they say the bear is thinking: *Send more tourists. The last ones were delicious.*"

I laughed. The postmark was Longmont, Colorado.

Edom went right to our bedroom. I sneaked up and watched her edge her shoebox out from under her bed and put her money in. Too bad, Edom. Orion and I were plenty used to digging out each other's secrets. I leaned in, startling her. "Did you steal that shoebox?" I asked.

She pushed it hastily back under. "Topher gave it to me."

I felt a tiny stab of jealousy, which was ridiculous.

"Come and eat," Mom called.

She'd spent some money at the farmers' market, and a vendor had tipped her with asparagus, which I told Edom was a vegetable that smells like old socks.

"All right," Mom said. "We've got to be eating some greens, though."

At the cabin Topher had showed us how to gather miner's lettuce growing in the wild. He was a handy guy—I had to give him that.

Later, I washed our dishes while Mom dried and

Edom counted her money in the living room. "Do you think Dad is really in Colorado?" I asked.

"Sure seems that way." Mom took my head and pulled it onto her shoulder. "He's probably thinking about us right now."

"I wish he'd come see us," I said. "Tell me a story about him."

"He didn't believe in birthday parties," Mom said, "but he did believe in taking a kid to a berry patch and letting her stick raspberries on her fingers. He didn't care about sticky spots on tutus. Fill up all ten fingers and eat them off and do it all over again." She held my hand up and kissed my fingers.

That night, Edom tossed and thrashed more than ever until I was dizzy with tiredness. "Edom," I said. "Go to sleep!"

I thought she would say, "I can't." Instead she said, "No." So loud that I jumped.

"Why not?"

She didn't answer.

I can't be your mom, I thought. *I'm not old enough*

and besides . . . well . . . I don't know how to do it.

I can't be your big sister, either.

I was always a little sister before.

I missed Orion so fiercely that even the blues weren't big enough to express it.

In the morning, when I woke up, Edom's bed was empty. Maybe I could catch her in the act of stealing. Dad used to say, "If you have to eat a toad, do it before breakfast and nothing worse will happen to you all day."

Outside, crows were hopping around in the mizzle and cawing at the top of their lungs. When I looked closer, I saw a heap of black feathers in the street. It was a pretty sad scene.

No Edom, though.

I walked around back. Under the drooping tree branches, I saw a flash of Edom's blue coat. As quietly as I could, I squelched through the yard and went in on my hands and knees.

Behind me, I could still hear the crows' mourning racket.

Edom's little moon face turned toward me, all

scared, but before I could say anything, a voice came from the next-door yard.

"Come out of there." It was a woman and, wow, did she sound mad!

Edom grabbed my arm.

"This time," the voice said. "No mercy for you."

Chapter Eighteen

Then the wife just to smell him popped up from the clothes,
When up got the crab-fish and nipped her by the nose.
Hey man and ho man, come hither, do you hear?
But the crab-fish was ready and caught him by the ear.

I peered frantically through the branches, trying to spot a glimpse of the woman in the next yard. Worst toad *ever*! "Back out," I mouthed to Edom.

"I can see you." The woman's voice was raspy and cold. "Don't think I can't."

Seriously? I pressed myself back into the branches. Why did Mom have to find Edom such a bright coat?

The woman started grumbling. Low. I gave Edom a nudge.

Frozen solid. And panic written on her face—with a big, fat marker.

Maybe she had stolen something really valuable. I nudged branches aside cautiously.

"Look." The voice was slightly more friendly. Tricky, maybe. "I like you. I've always liked you. But you won't stay in your own place."

What had Edom done? I felt the wet soaking through the knees of my pants.

"Who asked you to invite yourself into my yard?" Now the voice was really mean. "This means murder."

Edom squeaked.

Murder?

"You!"

Edom and I both jumped.

"You're dead. I've got you now."

Seriously? The wild thing in my chest was thumping away. Maybe she had something else in the yard that she was tormenting. A dog?

"Stop!" I shouted. I filled my lungs with air. "Wait!"

Dad's voice filled my mind. *That's my stout-hearted girl!* I fought the branches and stumbled forward. "Stop it right now!" My voice filled the galaxy. I felt my body go into fighting stance.

Except . . . the woman in front of me was sitting on a mobility scooter. Her wrinkled face was angry, and she was holding a sharp tool pointed at a hole in the ground. I'd stood up to bullies before. But . . . none of them had been this decrepit.

What was in that hole? A lizard? A snake?

I could feel drizzle dripping down my neck, turning me soggy. I wasn't about to give ground, though. She shouldn't be a bully even if she was disabled.

The woman lifted the stick. To spear me? Or in self-defense?

Behind me, I heard a rustling. Edom. That was brave of her—if not too smart. "Go home!" I said sharply, not daring to take my eyes off the woman.

Edom didn't move.

The woman lowered the stick. She leaned forward and I saw drops of mist on her glasses. "You aren't afraid of an old widow-woman on a garden buggy, are you?" She was trying to talk to Edom, who was standing right by my back pockets.

"We're not afraid," I said. Not like a dog or lizard or snake would be.

"So." The woman straightened out her sweater, calm now. "There are other early risers in this neighborhood. Besides Victor's chickens. I thought I was hearing things. Mind you, I don't like to come back to my house and discover all kinds of surprises. You two been next door all winter?" She gave me a sharp, suspicious look.

"I was living with Madam Marie and lots of other people," I said. Let her know I had plenty of backup. Never mind that they were miles away.

She took off her glasses and rubbed them. "All right. Call me Madam Backyardigan in my cardigan." She plucked at her sweater to make sure we knew what she meant by *cardigan* and then chuckled at her own joke. Then she glared back down at the hole. "It seems I missed out on plenty of neighborhood news." She put on her glasses and studied us sternly. "I thought that house back of me was scheduled to be scraped. Are you squatters?"

"No." I looked around. What a mess of a yard. Maybe *she* was a squatter.

She scowled. "My hip broke. Nasty customers took it as their invitation to move in and take over."

"We'll help you get the dog out of your yard," I said. Ivy was snaking over the roof of the shed and grass grew practically up to my waist. "You don't have to murder anything."

"Dogs have been around. Raccoons, too." Her voice got more accusing. "But it's these weeds I want to strangle."

"You're mean to plants," Edom said suddenly.

"Only the ones who are mean to me!" The woman reached down to touch something green. "Hello, hosta," she said. "Love the new leaves. Sorry the slugs got you so ratty."

I watched in astonishment.

"Trust me," she crooned. "It'll get better." She straightened up. "I don't suppose you two want a job."

A job? I beamed a charm-the-grown-up smile. I was prepared to do any kind of work to get Orion back.

"Kids these days like to sit and play with things that beep and whistle." She cracked her knuckles. "Are you strong enough to murder weeds?"

Edom squeaked.

"She's a friend of weeds," I said. "And she takes things very literally."

"Some of these nasty customers deserve no friends." Our neighbor looked grim. "Bindweed. Its roots can twist thirty feet down." She speared her long stick into the hole and lifted it. I saw a tangle of roots like white spaghetti.

"And that stinker over there flings its seeds ten feet in the air." Madam Backyardigan was getting more steamed by the second. "Canary reed grass took over my pond and ran off my Pacific tree frogs. You're not going to stick up for thugs, are you?"

"Blackberries are thugs," I said. "I'd never stick up for them." Edom started moving hastily back to the tree. She'd had enough.

"I'd like to put ivy and blackberries in a room and see who wins that fight!" The woman's expression reminded me of the crab-fish that nipped people's noses.

I wasn't easily intimidated, though. "One time, I helped my brother dig out a blackberry root that was so big I couldn't get my arms around it," I told her.

"You've got some tough in you, then." She started moving the motorized scooter forward—but the weeds stopped her. "I could give you a tryout with dandelions and let you show me what you're made of. That friend of yours might not be tough enough."

"She's my cousin," I said. Obviously, the woman didn't know her pots were gone. Yet. I'd tell her that Edom could pay for them out of her money.

Madam Backyardigan pointed her stick toward the fence. "What on God's green earth made dandelions think they were welcome? I'll pay you a nickel for every root. A dime if you get the whole thing. That bad customer will storm back if a tiny tip of it is left in the ground."

We were down to negotiations. "How about a dime per root and fifty cents if we get the whole thing?"

"A quarter for the whole thing. Final offer." She gave me a sharp look. "You won't get many. It won't hurt you to try, though. I'll get tools out of the shed. But I'd better not discover you're squatting next door or all bets are off."

If she went to the shed, she'd see the missing pots. "Just let me run back and talk to my mom about the job first."

I crawled through the branches of the tree to our

yard. Edom was staring at her toes on the back steps with her doll beside her. Wet and miserable. I went right up to her and stooped down until I was on her level.

"You want money, right?"

She nodded silently.

"I'll help, but we have to get clear with each other." I gave her a tough stare. "No stealing anything, including pots. What do you even want all the money for anyway?"

She pressed her lips together.

"If you're a thief or a selfish little hoarder, no one will hire you," I said sternly. "They won't even like you."

Edom folded her arms around her doll. "I don't care what you think!" she said. "Amy-mom likes me and she needs me."

"Sure," I said. "She needs for you to stay out of the way."

"How do you know?" She jumped to her feet and put her hands on her hips. "Who says? What makes you think you know so much?"

Huh. "I know she needs people who are experts and you're not a doctor," I said.

Edom stamped her foot. "I'm not a doctor but I'm

not rubbish. I need to go there and be with her."

"Well, I never said you were rubbish." We stared at each other, eyeball-to-eyeball. "How do you think you're going to get all the way from Portland to California?" I asked.

The punch went out of her. "How do *you* get places?" she asked.

"Paddy Wagon."

She began to rock herself and the doll. Behind her glasses, her eyes were brown and sad. She wasn't big enough to be one of Jupiter's moons. Maybe she was that comet that almost smashed into Jupiter. Or I was like a migrating bird and she was an ant.

"Sometimes we use a Greyhound bus," I finally said.

"Could I earn enough for the bus?" she asked. "If we get the job? And if we get to the recyclables before anyone else does?"

Pow! Like the song says, "I saw the light!"

Perfect!

She and I both wanted our freedom from this place.

"Of course," I said. "I'll help you. We could do something at the farmers' market to earn money." Something better than the twins' gig.

Edom nodded nervously. It was like the day the collie pup suddenly stuck its nose into Orion's hand.

"You also have to put some money in the food envelope," I said sternly. "And I'll be putting some of my money into my Paddy Wagon fund."

She bobbed her head yes. The top of her hair was getting messy. Mom's braids weren't tight the way Amymom's had been. I could hug her but it would be like hugging an artichoke. I shook her hand instead. "Deal!" I said.

No need to tell Mom until Edom and I presented her with money for three Greyhound tickets and told her it was time for movin' on. Mom wouldn't want to let her precious Edom go, but I'd figure out some way to persuade her.

I felt like singing at the top of my lungs.

I'm a one-way train,
Rattling down the track.
You can come along, along.
But I'm not coming back.

Chapter Nineteen

Yo, heave ho! Raise her from below.
The anchor's off the ground
And we are outward bound.

By the time we filled Mom in about the job offer and ate breakfast and put on old jeans, I was all jazzed up and ready to pop. Unless our neighbor got super mad about the pots, we had a plan. Yard work? Seriously? How bad could it be?

Mom walked us around the long way—so she didn't have to crawl under tree branches—to inspect the job site. We passed a man pushing a little boy in a stroller with a girl running behind. "Going to the park," the boy told us.

"That's how I do my ballet, Daddy," the girl kept saying. "That's how I do my ballet." The daddy was all shrunken into himself like he had too much on his mind. I wanted to run after them and tell the little girl I would watch her do her ballet.

"So sorry about your hip," Mom told our neighbor first thing. "This yard is a big job."

Our neighbor's grumpy walrus look faded as she talked about her plants. "I moved here about fifteen years ago when my husband died," she told Mom, "and believe me this place was tragic. Ivy and bindweed climbing up the trees. Blackberries blocking the shed door. The only thing that gave me hope was the sound of Pacific tree frogs nearby." She gave us a fierce look. "That's what steams me the most. Pond dried up and clogged with weeds."

How steamed would she be about Edom stealing? My smile felt tight.

"When I moved in, friends gave me roses and blueberries and flowering trees. Look at my dearies." She waved at the yard. "How they suffered without me."

I showed Edom the spot where dandelions had helped themselves to the soil in a lizard-shaped mass.

"Watch your step, there," our neighbor said. "The French and Italians and Spanish and Portuguese and Germans all call that monster by the same name. *Tooth*"—her voice went low and creepy—"*of the lion*. They gobbled up my rosemary and tansy and took no prisoners."

If wolves ever napped with the lambs, maybe dandelions would make peace with the tansy. For now, I thought, good impression before confession.

I got the tools and explained the pay system to Edom—a dime for a partial and a quarter for the whole thing. "I had practice digging at Rainbow Farm," I said. "Stand back and watch." I stabbed a trowel into the dirt. Did leftover tips of dandelion root squirm their way up through the soil until they got back to the top? "This is one quarter I can definitely get."

Behind us, Madam Backyardigan told Mom, "My granddaughter owns the bee box over there. What makes her think I want those stingers so close when I can't even outrun them?"

Jessica, the defender of bees, Victor had said. Where was Jessica?

I pushed my fingers deep into the soil around the dandelion root and glanced up to make sure Edom was watching. I gave a mighty tug. *For Paddy Wagon fund and the Greyhound plan!*

Pop.

This was one quarter I definitely couldn't get.

Edom didn't laugh at me. She just crouched down by her own dandelion.

Soon my back hurt. I kept sneezing dirt out my nose. Seriously annoying! I let out a growl of frustration.

"Don't lose heart," Madam Backyardigan called. "Sometimes the best we can do is slow those bad characters down." She and Mom had uncovered a strawberry patch. "My darlings, my treasures," she crooned. "And look! They're ripe! Help yourself to all you want."

Food we didn't have to buy. "How are you doing?" I asked Edom.

She tipped her bucket so I could see.

"Wow," I said. "You are great at this."

"Mr. Lion Teeth," she said. "Amy-mom and I went on a safari in Kenya, and I saw lions under a tree. When one yawned, I saw its teeth."

Huh! The artichoke was shedding its prickles.

Edom held up a smooth, oval rock. "We could sell potatoes at the farmers' market." She uncurled her other fist and I saw a smaller oval. "And eggs."

"We can't sell rocks and pretend they're eggs and potatoes," I said. "The minute someone bites into one . . ."

Wait. Edom's mouth turned up. She was making a joke.

She could joke!

Mom came over. "I have an idea to check out," she said. "You'll be right here?"

I gave her thumbs-up.

Madam Backyardigan went back to conversing with her plants. "I apologize," I heard her say. "I had to abandon you to that horrid yellow archangel that sucked up all the nutrients."

I shoved the trowel in. My arms itched, but Edom was humming. Did she have eyes in her fingers? "You seem like an expert or something," I said.

"I helped my grandmother. In Ethiopia." She uncurled her hand and showed me a worm.

"Dead," I said.

She shook her head. "It's only playing dead."

Sure enough, a second later the worm twisted and wriggled. "Bring that baby here," Madam Backyardigan called. A minute later, the two of them were looking into the compost bin with interest.

I got up, too. I should be paddleboarding with Orion and Dad, out in the waves with the salt sparkling on my arms. I should be traveling the Oregon coast, where anything could be turned into a festival. Crayfish. Kites. Classical music and Celtic music and blues and BBQ.

I'd traded in ocean views for rotting garbage.

As we watched, the worm wriggled down into leaves and coffee grounds and eggshells and banana peels and even an old sweater. Its tail disappeared last. According to *National Geographic,* it would eat leaves and roots and garbage all the way down.

"Something smells bad," I said. "Let's get back to work."

I took a few steps. And a few more. "Ugh." I said. "It smells bad everywhere."

"Dogs doing their business." Madam Backyardigan shook her head. "You can help me clean it up. If we see any of that nasty raccoon scat, though, let me handle it."

"What's scat?" Edom asked.

On the way back to the dandelions, I told her about the coyote scat Orion and I had seen at the edge of a dirt road in California—with the hair and bones of its prey in it. "Hey." I held my nose. "That smell is here, too. I didn't notice it before. Scat must be all over this yard."

"You're the smelly one." Edom pointed. "I think it's on your shoe."

I lifted my foot. "Ugh!" I shouted.

"Jupiter stepped in poopiter," Edom told Madam Backyardigan.

Wow. It took me about fifteen minutes to get the scat off my shoe, and instead of sympathy or help, all I got was laughter. What kind of work conditions had I gotten myself into, anyway?

Chapter Twenty

In eighteen hundred and forty-five,
I thought myself more dead than alive,
I thought myself more dead than alive
While working on the railway.

"I haven't laughed this hard since before I broke my hip," Madam Backyardigan said.

"Thanks a lot," I said. But I couldn't stay mad. Maybe the boss lady would still be in a good mood when I confessed about the pots.

You make your own luck, buskers said, and you keep your eyes open for any luck lying around that you might be able to scoop up. Sometimes you waited for your luck to turn. "What time should we start tomorrow?" I asked. *Nail down a commitment.*

Madam Backyardigan chuckled. "I'm an early riser. Me and my buggy."

"Why do you call it a buggy?" Edom asked.

"Would you rather call it my chariot?" She laughed and patted the scooter.

Time to swallow my tough beans. "I'll put the tools in the shed," I said. Cucumber cool. "And then I think we should talk terms."

"Terms, is it?" she asked.

I nodded. *Jupiter, you are smart and fearless and you will be perfect.* I marched around the corner of the shed. And . . . stopped.

Right by the door I saw piles of little pots. "Take to recycling" was scrawled on a piece of cardboard.

Embarrassing! Why did Edom have to be so private?

Inside the shed, a drawing of a goat was pinned to the wall. Under the goat, someone had scribbled, "I feel totally different about things now. Thank you for the sock tea, Goat Girl."

Well, I felt totally different, too. I went spinning out like the giant, bold, third-brightest object in the night sky that I was, and Madam Backyardigan fell right into my orbit.

Starting tomorrow, she agreed, she'd pay us by the hour, not by the dandelion.

We would clean up scat, and pull weeds from around the poor choking plants, and carry stuff around front to the recycling and yard waste bins. "Do you care if we help ourselves to some of those pots by the shed?" I asked. "For the farmers' market?"

"Be my guest." She counted out our pay. Four dollars for me. Seven for Edom. "Fill them with raspberry suckers if you like. Next year this time, you'll have your own raspberries."

Next year this time, Orion and Mom and I would be aboard Paddy Wagon meandering up Highway 101 from California to Oregon, hearing a burble and a splash a minute before we saw a waterfall pouring over the rocks. We'd drive through pine trees where the sky looked like a thin slice of blue far above. Four dollars wasn't going to get too far on repairing Paddy Wagon. But opportunity was knocking.

Back in our house, I put two dollars in the food

envelope and two under my pillow to start the Paddy Wagon fund. Mom had cooked macaroni and cheese, and we had berries for a feast. "Perfect!" she said when I told her about our new job. She was spiky with confidence. "*I* managed to connect with my roommate from when I was in college. Cassandra. She's going to help me with a surprise for us."

A friend of Mom's might be able to do anything. Build a boat. Play the piccolo. Weave a hammock with her teeth. "What?" I said. "Tell me!"

Mom danced around the mostly empty living room singing a silly song she made up on the spot about finding thrills on strawberry hills. "I'm not telling," she said, laughing.

I grabbed her hand and we boogied and shimmied and swung. We danced the Car Wash and the Achy Breaky and the Cotton-Eyed Joe. "I'm still not telling," she said, laughing more.

Good. Because I wasn't ready to tell her about my new grand plan yet, either.

Edom climbed onto the couch, piling quarters into shiny towers on the wooden arms.

"You and Edom will be okay next door tomorrow while I check this out, right?" Mom dipped me.

"Madam said we can use her bathroom if we don't want to come back to our house," Edom said shyly.

I could feel my ponytail flying. We were so out of here! By the fourth of July I'd be singing my lungs out while fireworks rained yellow and red and silver down on all the tourists at Yaquina Bay.

Chapter Twenty-One

Oats, peas, beans, and barley grow.
Oats, peas, beans, and barley grow.
Whether you like it or whether you know
Oats, peas, beans, and barley grow.

The first week of garden work was damp with bursts of rain. Every afternoon, when we decided we couldn't work another second, I looked like the algae Topher had showed me when we stayed in the cabin—brown slime in the mountain stream.

It was called rock snot.

Exactly how I felt on our new job.

After Edom and I got cleaned up, we'd go with Mom to find useful things. One afternoon, we figured out the buses to see the St. Johns Bridge, the prettiest of all. The day Madam had a physical therapy appointment, Mom took us to Union Station to walk on a pedestrian bridge. When we got to the middle, she showed us how to jump ten times in unison and then freeze perfectly still.

The whole, long bridge danced and trembled under us. We all looked at each other and started laughing. "I can't believe we're making it bounce!" Edom said.

"My friends, you've just experienced the boing-boing bridge," Mom said.

That day was like the best family times in my old orbit.

In the evenings, while Mom played her cello, Edom and I sat on the front porch and watched the parade of people out and about in the neighborhood. Crows gathered close because Edom tended to drop things they liked to eat. A guy passed us rapping softly. Words seemed to float around him like *move* and *prove*, *learning* and *burning*, *in you* and *continue*.

The next week, temperatures climbed into the eighties, and at work, we went from damp to dusty. Like someone turned off a spigot, just the way Victor said. We had to open our windows to sleep. But parts of Madam's yard looked like swirls of color, and the first raspberry I ate burst in my mouth giving me jolts of joy.

Edom took to everything. Even slug patrol. Every morning, she and Madam turned over boards and pots and grapefruit halves and scooped slugs into a bucket. Most had pulled their little ear things in and looked like pebbles. If you held them on your palm, they lengthened out again and started to crawl.

"Ugh," I said.

"I don't judge them for their slime," Edom said.

"Fine," I said. "Judge them for their 27,000 teeth that can chomp everything."

I helped Edom carry the bucket of slugs across the street to dump into Victor's chicken house. The hens set up a great cackling.

"Slugs are like ice cream for chickens," Edom said.

I wanted ice cream. Too bad it didn't come in a family box from the Food Bank. Sisters of the Open Road Café also gave meals, in barter for volunteer work, but Mom and I agreed that downtown place was too intense for Edom. Mom went by herself when Edom and I were on the job.

Mom was drinking a lot of coffee these days.

A *lot* of coffee.

Both Tuesdays, Edom and I beat the competition to the neighborhood redeemables. I added money to the food envelope and to my Paddy Wagon fund and gave Edom hers to put in her shoebox. We sat on the front porch and watched the THINK GREEN, THINK CLEAN truck come by with its claws to pick up the recycling bins and dump them.

Then we went right back to battling weeds. Public Enemy Number Three, according to Madam, was ivy. Edom and I lugged bags of it to the green bin labeled Portland Composts! "Jessica's friend from the No Ivy League said ivy is so evil we shouldn't put it in the compost bin," Madam told us. "Are you kidding me? Portland's composting facility can handle steak bones and pizza boxes but not ivy?"

We were *not* going to haul all that ivy out of the compost bin. Where was Jessica, anyway? Why didn't she come help lug and weed?

Public Enemy Number Two was bindweed with its spaghetti roots. Close behind in badness was the plant

Madam called Creeping Charlie and Edom called Long Finger. Her first word picture.

The soil was folding itself more tightly around all the roots, and Madam started hurrying us to get weeding done. "What's Public Enemy Number One?" I asked while Edom was pulling grass from around a rose bush.

Madam sniffed. "Public Enemy Number One isn't a plant."

I lifted my ponytail from my sweaty neck. "You mean it's a human?"

Madam sniffed again. "When it behaves itself, it is."

"Who is it?" I asked.

She only shot me a grumpy walrus I-don't-want-to-discuss-it look. Maybe I should give her the rest of the blessed thistle.

"Stop poking me!" Edom shouted at the bush. "I'm only trying to help you."

"Plants can hear you," I told her. Scientists played recorded sounds to make a mustard plant think a caterpillar was chewing nearby, and the plant created mustard oil to defend itself. *National Geographic News.*

"Now these stinkers . . ." Madam reached her long forked stick into a weedy spot. "They might hear me coming but they can't get away." She waved an oxalis plant in the air. "And they can't hide. Not with those yellow flowers."

Without flowers, oxalis could be sneakier. But without flowers it couldn't attract pollinators. Like it was supereasy for Orion and me to blend into crowds and avoid police who liked to hassle buskers—but unfortunately we needed to attract attention to busk.

I tugged handfuls of a weed that came up with the sound of stitches ripping out, while Edom toured the yard with Madam. "Is this a nasty customer?" she asked, pointing.

"California poppy," Madam said. "Jessica says it's a joy to bees and butterflies. It's a party animal, I'll give you that. Flinging its seeds around like it owns the place."

Edom looked like a small detective with her glasses and serious expression. "Is *that* a nasty customer?"

"Bronze fennel. It'll use its licorice smell to try to fool you into keeping it around. Give it the stink-eye and dig it right out. That over there is maidenhair vine. All curly like your hair."

All messy like your hair, I thought.

"What's that?" Edom asked.

Madam Backyardigan chuckled. "That's a stump."

"Beside the stump, I mean."

Madam Backyardigan maneuvered her scooter, trying to see. "I'm not sure. Let's tie it up and see what it eats."

"But it doesn't eat," Edom said.

"That was my father's expression when something puzzled him," Madam said.

Sweat and sunscreen ran down my forehead and into my eyes. Oh, for the chill of an ocean wave!

"What's that?" Edom asked.

"It's mine," a voice said. Jessica was leaning against the corner of the house with a turquoise skateboard under her arm. "It's a home for mason bees." Jessica stretched out her calves like a runner warming up. "I made it from the hollow stalks of Joe-Pye weed. In science class. Free. No money spent at all. You know, Grandma, without pollinators like those bees, your berry and flower blossoms will shrivel up and drop off."

"I don't want bees brawling in my yard," Madam said.

"Don't worry." Jessica came into the yard. "My science teacher says honeybees and mason bees don't interact at all."

Madam sniffed. "High school science teachers are tree huggers," she said.

Jessica's face relaxed into a grin. "I'm a tree hugger, Grandma. You have a tree hugger staying in your back bedroom."

Madam ignored that. "She wants me to uproot my roses and daylilies and put in a rain garden," she told us. "Trying to convince me I don't know my own mind. Exactly like her dad."

"Why do you need to grow rain?" Edom asked.

Jessica stuck her hands in her pockets. "Think about how many times I've taken your side, Grandma. You need to let me have my way sometimes." She moved close to me. "You can eat those dandelion leaves, you know."

Madam Backyardigan dug a packet of seeds out of

her garden bag and tossed it to Jessica. "If you want something to eat, plant these carrots. Dig a nice straight row."

Jessica tore open the packet and flung a handful of seeds into the air. "Run!" she shouted. "Run free while you have a chance!"

Madam sniffed. I tried not to laugh. "My brother has a girlfriend with the same name as you," I told her.

"Of all the girls born in my year, 78 percent were named Jessica." She called over to her grandmother, "Did you know Portland has the world record for tree hugging? Nine-hundred-and-fifty-one people all hugged a tree at the same time."

She probably argued with her grandma more than 78 percent of the girls born that year. No exaggeration . . . or almost none.

Jessica turned to go.

Stop her! "Did you say you can eat dandelions?" I asked.

She came over to me. "See that little one? Stir-fry it with olive oil and some bacon and you have a meal."

"Too bad we don't have any bacon," I said.

"I have something," Edom said.

"Oh sure," I said. "Ha-ha."

"I do." She looked satisfied. "Pepperoni."

Jessica dug a crumpled paper bag out of her backpack. "Fill this with young dandelion leaves. Meet you in your kitchen in five minutes—is the door unlocked?"

"The back one is. Or come around front and knock."

"Great," she said. "And call me Jess so nobody confuses me with any other Jessica."

I gave her a juicy smile. If I could make friends with Jess, it wouldn't take me long to be soaring on that skateboard.

Chapter Twenty-Two

Shoo fly, don't bother me.
Shoo fly, don't bother me.
Shoo fly, don't bother me,
For I belong to somebody.
I feel, I feel, I feel, I feel like the morning star.
I feel, I feel, I feel, I feel like the morning star.

Madam Backyardigan shook her head. "You leave me out of that kind of foolishness," she said. I put away our tools seriously fast. When we were walking through our own backyard, Edom said, "Your mom can have her wish of eating something green." She looked up at me through her little round glasses. "What if you had one wish and it could really happen?"

Instant money, I thought as I went up the back steps. Or for Dad to come have adventures with us. "You should wish for a new doll," I told Edom. "That one is pathetic."

She picked it up. "Other kids walked by her, you know. They whispered that another girl would take her home. But no one ever did. It was my superpower to take her home."

Sometimes talking to Edom made me feel small. To make up for it, I said, "We need to find someone with the superpower to help with your hair."

"I like my hair," she said. "It's unique."

"Of course it is," I said. "But Mom doesn't know how to braid it that well."

In the kitchen, I got out pans while Edom found the stick of pepperoni. "Cut the pieces big," she said. "So I can pick them out of mine. In case it's pork."

I'd gone to school with Muslim kids and they were always careful about not getting any pork on them. "Are you Muslim?" I asked her.

"I'm Orthodox."

Someone knocked on the front door. "Who is it?" I shouted.

"Open up." It was Jess.

I unlocked the door. "Well, you could have been an intruder."

"Sure," Jess said. "But you could be one of those ants that gloms onto any intruder that gets into its space and then explodes." She handed something to me. "Your mail."

Score!

A postcard from Dad *and* a package with Orion's looping handwriting. Nothing for Edom—for once.

I showed Jess the kitchen and then sat down with my loot. The postcard was of a bull with ferocious-looking horns. On the back Dad had written, "Today I saw a sign that said, 'Do not cross this field unless you can do it in 9.9 seconds. The bull can do it in 10.'" The postmark was Longmont, Colorado, again.

Inside Orion's package I found a flat black phone.

Dear Jupiter,

Topher brought this to the café. Hang on there. Don't judge me. He was heading up to Portland for a job and he's a little worried about Edom and wanted you and Mom to know he's close by if he can help out. But he said I should mail it to show you he's serious about not gonna barge in or anything. It's got 30 minutes of talk *and some phone numbers in there. In case you need anything. You don't have to call me. Or him. Or 911. Or anyone. But don't be stubborn if you need to. It's not a sign of weakness or anything.*

Orion

The words wiggled into my brain like exploding ants. Why did Topher think Edom was his business? I scrolled down to the café number.

"Yo ho ho," Orion answered. "You guys okay?" He sounded nervous. "I can't tie up this phone, but—"

"Sorry," I said quickly. "We're fine." I paused. "How's Jessica?"

"She's . . . um." I heard the clinking of glasses in the background. "She has a boyfriend."

"Oh."

"It isn't me."

Whoa, Nellie! If I were on a gallows cold I wouldn't want to count on anyone but Orion. "Sorry," I said again—and I sort of was, for his sake. "Hey, something good is happening. But don't get your hopes up quite yet."

"Okay." Orion laughed. "This is me dialing back my hopes."

"About Topher . . . you know we don't need him coming to our rescue or something!"

"He said he's been hired to do a painting," Orion said—too quickly.

"I'll refresh the blessed thistle," I said. "And I'll call you again soon."

I put the phone under my pillow. In the kitchen, Jess was chopping garlic. She waved the knife at me. "I've been telling your sister about invasive plants." She grinned at Edom. "Hey. Thanks for listening, dude."

"She's my cousin," I said. "And by the way, I know one invasive really well. Rock snot." Also, Topher was also like an invasive species, refusing to stay gone for good. I closed my eyes and breathed in. Onion. Garlic. The summery sweat and stem-and-leaves smell of Jess, skateboarding, tree-hugging defender of bees. "Can I use your phone to check on something?" I asked.

The Greyhound site was simple to find, but different days had different prices. Three tickets would cost around three hundred dollars.

Was there a kid fare?

I skimmed and clicked. There. Twenty percent

discount. Not much, but it was something.

Edom wouldn't be coming back, though. How much for one way?

The front door opened. "Hello?" Mom called. I quickly handed the phone back to Jess.

"Surprise!" Edom and I shouted together without any planning. We looked at each other and suddenly we were laughing. But part of my brain was thinking about all those dollars for tickets. How many weeds would we have to pull, anyway?

Chapter Twenty-Three

From Austin town we sailed away, heave away, Santyano,
Round Cape Horn to 'Frisco bay and we're bound for Californio.
And it's heave her up, and away we'll go, heave away, Santyano,
Heave her up and away we'll go, and we're bound for Californio.

Mom came rushing in like a whirlwind of enthusiasm. "Surprise back!" She laughed with us and tipped open the canvas bags she was carrying. Out tumbled apples and bananas and cans of tomato paste and some bags marked "pizza dough."

It turned out Mom's friend Cassandra didn't make hammocks with her teeth.

She was an urban food forager who knew about a pizza place closing shop.

"Is that the same as a dumpster diver?" I asked.

"Not according to Cassandra," Mom said. Cassandra called herself all kinds of things including a vegan freegan, a clean diver, and an anthropologist of food waste—but not a dumpster diver. "What's happening here?"

I filled Mom in. Jess gave the pan a little shake and turned off the stove. I handed forks around.

"Ready," Jess said. "Set. Taste."

I looked at Mom as I chewed. We swallowed in unison. "Bitter!" we said together. It made me laugh so hard I spit little bits of green.

"But in a really great, radsy way," Jess said. "Right?" *Radsy* was skateboard talk.

"Does anyone mind," I asked, "if we also make a pizza?" Without waiting for an answer, I started spreading the loot on the counter.

Jess did her best to pep talk dandelions. "You know what?" she said. "In science class we made a salad with 125 ingredients. Eating can be an adventure for your mouth. All kinds of tastes! Including fuzzy! Slimy!"

Ummm . . . no.

"I like the taste," Edom said. Maybe it reminded her of something she ate in Africa. Maybe our food was weird to Edom. I'd never considered that before.

Mom and I started moving fast in perfect sync, proving if we could get to busking, we'd be great. Like the two sisters Lennon and Maisy, slapping cups and singing "Call Your Girlfriend" in sweet harmony when Maisy was a little kid. All we needed was a YouTube video that got eighteen-million hits.

Then fixing Paddy Wagon would be easy.

When the pizza was baked and the dandelion greens were in a dish and Jess had run next door for more strawberries—and to make sure Madam wasn't going to change her mind and come eat with us—we spread out free fabric as a picnic cloth on the living room floor. "This evening," Mom said, "we celebrate abundance and generosity and good neighbors."

Mom liked having a team. So different from Dad and me, who were unbound, nomad planets that free-float through the Milky Way. No gravity tugging us down.

Edom and Madam Backyardigan were earth people,

of course. Diggers. People who hid things in shoeboxes and stumps.

Whose camp was Jess in?

Mine! I decided. She wanted adventures—even for her mouth.

"Dig in," Mom said.

I had to show Jess how much we were alike. I piled my plate with dandelion greens and took a bunch of small bites and chewed as fast as I could, which sort of made my mouth numb and helped me keep going even though, honestly, dandelions were worse than asparagus. No exaggeration!

Edom slurped her milk through a straw, sounding like the ocean gurgling up to a rock.

"Cassandra set me up with an all-day job," Mom said. "I'll be laying tile in a kitchen—two weeks from now. It doesn't exactly use my building skills, but it'll pay good money."

"Mom can build houses," I told Jess.

She glanced at my greens and gave me two thumbs up. "Way better than my summer job as a barista," she said. "I wish I knew how to do things around my grandma's house."

I thought about what Madam had said. "Can your dad help?" I asked.

Jess shook her head. "He'd take it as proof that Grandma shouldn't even be trying to live there anymore."

Mom smiled at Jess. "How about you watch Jupiter and Edom while I lay tile? It'll be a marathon day." She rubbed her lower back like it was already stiff. "Then I'll do some work for your grandma. Sound like a swap?"

Opportunity knocking! I put my hands together to say please to Jess. "Can I try your skateboard?" I asked. "I've done it before. In California." I imagined myself doing a kickflip. Live to skate to live.

Jess turned to Edom. "What about you? What do you like to do for fun?"

Edom crossed her arms. "I only want to make money."

"I've got a good idea for making a bunch of money at the farmers' market on Saturday," I told her. I took another bite of dandelion to impress Jess. "By the way, I never met my grandparents. Do you mind if we're helping your grandma?"

"Course not." Jess looked down. "I'm just scared she'll get her hopes up and then find out she can't make it all alone next year when I have to move back in with Dad."

"Did you know you have scat in your yard?" Edom asked.

Jess grinned at her. "Did *you* know some birds carry scat from their nests and stick it in nearby trees."

"Gross! Why?"

"To distract predators. Baby birds don't wear diapers, you know." Edom giggled.

"Some caterpillars fling their scat—which is called *frass*, by the way—far away from them for the same reason," Jess said. "Pretty chill, huh?" She turned to me. "Maybe you two can kinda borrow my grandma for a while. I know she likes you."

It was hard to imagine the boss lady as a cozy grandma.

After supper, while Jess took Mom to talk with Madam about the house, I dug through the Miscellaneous box for the tambourine. "Here," I told Edom. "This is how you grip the shell."

"What?" She sounded horrified.

"The farmers' market," I said. "Remember? The bus tickets?"

Good one. She reluctantly curled her hand around the tambourine. I showed her how to tap and roll. "Not bad," I said. "Next time, we'll work on how to tingle."

"Do you really think we can get money?" she asked.

"Of course."

When we went to bed that night, I asked, "Want me to tell you a story?"

"About the plan," Edom said.

I stared into the darkness, thinking. A train whistle moaned with that high, lonesome sound Dad loved.

Why did I even need Mom to go along? Would it be so hard to handle sitting for about twenty hours on a Greyhound bus?

Great idea! Edom and I could go alone!

Wait. Impossible.

But why? Dad had always taught Orion and me lots and lots of things about being self-sufficient.

Suddenly, I was sure. I could do this! I tried to think through the steps.

"Okay," I said. I started with the number eight city bus. A dollar twenty-five for a kid to ride. "Do you remember that the Greyhound station is right by the train station and the boing-boing bridge?"

"I remember," she whispered in the dark.

I figured it out step by step. We could ask a friendly adult if we could travel with her. We'd try to get a whole row so we could spread out and take turns with the window seat on the ocean side in case something like a whale floated by.

"What if someone tries to stop us?" Edom asked.

"Orion and I came up with lots of ways to avoid anyone who tried to hassle us," I said. "If you see someone in a uniform, hide."

"Okay," Edom whispered.

"The first thing is always locate your safe spaces," I said. My brain was bubbling. Some people sang mournfully about walking this lonesome valley all by yourself, but Dad and I knew we didn't need anyone to help us figure out our way. This was one awesomesauce new idea—and no exaggeration.

Chapter Twenty-Four

Hard Times, hard times, come again no more
Many days you have lingered around my cabin door;
Oh! Hard times come again no more.

The next morning, the more I thought about how proud Dad would be of my adventure, the more my mind became a rocket ship of ideas. First, more money. I decided "Hard Times Come Again No More" would be our first farmers' market act. Lennon and Maisy used it for a YouTube video before they got famous.

Now that I had the grand plan to think about, it was easy to feel, feel, feel like the morning star even though Edom and Madam and I were hot, hot, hot. Then we got sudden drenching rains that made us grimy, grimy, grimy—so grimy that one day when Mom put together an Ikea bookshelf for some cash, she stopped by a dentist office and got a free toothbrush to help Edom and me clean the soil out from under our fingernails. "I'm not spending one cent I don't have to," Mom said. "I might have to buy you rain boots if this weather keeps up. And it's time to do laundry."

We also had to save up for utilities. And we still didn't have much furniture. A few times, Victor had driven Mom downtown so she could busk with her cello, but she said the competition was tough. The whole thing was giving her worry lines.

Too bad I couldn't tell her that soon I'd be solving everything.

On Thursday afternoon, Madam decided it was time to tackle the canary reed grass. We dug as deeply as we could into the dry pond and put down black plastic. "High temperatures are back tomorrow," Madam said. "Got to count on the sun to fry the roots of this bad character."

On Friday, before the farmers' market gig, Edom

and I filled thirty small black pots with raspberry suckers and arranged them in the wagon. Edom watered them. "I know it's hard to leave your home," she sang. "So drink some water, little honey-o." The hose hissed.

Madam was surveying the baby tomato plants Edom and I had just planted for her. I yawned. Why wouldn't Edom sleep? Why wasn't she tired? *I* was. I watched her lean over the compost bin and haul the ratty sweater out. "Put that back," I called.

Instead, she tucked it around a rose bush. "There," she told it. "Now no more complaining."

I laughed. It was weird to think that soon we'd never see this yard again.

Or Madam.

Or each other.

Think about California dreaming. Humming wheels and the road snaking along. Harbor seals sunning on the rocks. *Think about busking.* According to Mom, I was four when I stood beside Orion at a roadside stop, as bold as a new penny. "I sound very pretty when I'm singing," I'd announced. It had been a lucrative busking day.

Tomorrow would be, too.

The money would roll in, and then—we'd be on our way to adventure! *O my brother,* I thought. *You better not have forgotten how to be free. I'll be a burr in your fur until you remember.*

Edom shrieked.

I jumped.

"Bee!" Edom danced around squealing.

It was as huge and loud as a buzz saw. A *mutant* bee! Edom dropped the hose that flipped and flapped, and suddenly the world was all splashing and splattering with Edom and me yelping and hopping around.

Madam hollered something. I grabbed the hose.

Then I saw. It was a hummingbird, beating its wings so fast they buzzed.

It came so close I could swear it was studying me with one eye. As we gaped, dripping, it perched on a tomato cage for a few seconds. Then it was gone.

"Hummingbirds are the only type of bird that can fly backward," I told them. *National Geographic.*

That night, Mom sang while she knelt by the bathtub and detangled Edom's hair using coconut oil and her fingers. "No shampoo for your sweet head," she said. She had talked to a beauty shop about Ethiopian hair—and she'd taken notes. Rinse in filtered water. Use a conditioner about once a week.

When it came to Edom, Mom's soft heart would always get the best of her. That's why it was up to me to help Edom get back to California. "Looks good," I said. "Fluffy. Can I pat it?"

"I'm not a puppy." She frowned. "Did you learn about braiding, too?" she asked Mom.

"Hey." I gave Edom a big smile. "You tell Jess you want to go skateboarding the day Mom works on her tile job, and after we're done we can go to an Ethiopian restaurant. I bet someone there will know how to do good braids."

"Really? You know where one is?"

"Really."

She looked skeptical. "With *injera*?"

"Whatever that is," I said. "I'm sure they'll speak to you in Ethiopian."

She gave me the old look of scorn. "Ethiopian isn't a language."

"But will you?" I asked.

"Deal!" she said, looking at me as if I were the sun.

I went in the bedroom and studied my postcards, letting the infinite possibilities wash over the surface of Planet Jupiter.

Chapter Twenty-Five

Orphan children sees a hard time in this world.
Sister does the best she can,
But she don't really understand.
Orphan children sees a hard time in this world.

The next morning, I picked out a cute pair of pants with hearts on the pockets for Edom. I looped on my best beads. Dress to impress—especially those so-called twins. I even helped Edom decorate her doll with scraps of fabric. "Remember," I told her. "Make eye contact. Good customer service. And when we do our act, smile!"

She gave me a smile to demonstrate.

Pho-*ny*.

"Kind of like that," I said. "Only better." I knew the signs of getting nervous. "Here's what you do," I told her. "Stick out your tongue. Now leave it stuck out and count to ten. I'll do it with you."

Before we got to five, we were both giggling, and it was an actual good warm-up and no exaggeration.

I put our supplies in my daypack, and we pulled the wagonful of pots to the car, where we found Victor showing Mom an Oregon sunstone. "It glows from the inside," he said. "Why would anyone give his sweetheart a diamond—so unoriginal—when you could give a rock born in a volcano right from the good U S of A?"

I handed him a raspberry plant. "For you," I said. "Next summer, you can share raspberries with the chickens. Is it okay to take my wagon again?"

"I don't see why not." He hustled across the street to put his new plant in the shade.

Edom and I took our usual seats. "Why is he talking to you about sweethearts?" I asked Mom.

"We were comparing notes on how we've messed up." She smiled.

Gravity alert! "Do you like him?" I asked.

"Victor?" She laughed. "Not like that."

"So are you missing Dad?" I asked. *Please, please say yes.*

"Ah, the Prince of Adventure." Now her voice was affectionate. "I was lucky. . . ." This time she said it. "He stayed much longer than he'd planned and left behind the two things I'll always pack up and take with me—a constellation and a planet." She reached back and squeezed my arm. "No matter what happens with Topher, I won't ever forget that."

"What do you mean? What would happen?"

"Oh, you know." She laughed her famous Mom laugh and then Victor was back, and I knew Mom wouldn't say anything more.

But I sat there thinking, Help! Meteors crashing! Bits of matter flying everywhere!

I had to tell Dad to come visit and that it was really, really important. About two blocks from the farmers' market, I spotted a post office. Okay! Post offices could be very resourceful in getting mail to the rightful owner.

As soon as we got to Mom's spot, she was approached by some new fans, so I hustled myself and Edom to our spot, and pulled the tambourine and the beanbags and the lucky hat out of the daypack.

What *did* Mom mean about Topher?

Couldn't think about that now. *Get it together, Jupiter.* I took a deep breath. "Ready?"

"No!" Edom barely choked out the word.

"You'll be okay." I held out the tambourine. "Look—hardly anyone's here yet. Start tapping and the confidence will come right along."

Edom crossed her arms.

"We want to get people's attention," I said. "Before Mom gets playing. We can do an encore when she's taking a break."

Edom crouched, wrapping her arms around her knees.

I got right down beside her. "Don't you want money for getting to Amy-mom? Find someone friendly to look at. Like . . ." I looked around desperately.

Uh-oh.

Danielle was zooming our way. She had on a yellow-and-black headband with antennae sticking up. Moria was right behind, wearing green spider-web tights and lime-colored sneaks. If they were twins, why didn't their names rhyme? "The shade of this tree is good," Moria said, glancing at me. "If you don't mind."

"I do mind!" I said. "We were starting something."

"No, we weren't," Edom whispered.

"Come on!" I pounded my fist on the ground like a big baby.

"You do it." She sounded pitiful. "Maybe I will after that."

"Fine." I stood up. People were basically pouring into the farmers' market now. Any second now my mojo would kick in, and I'd shine like a sparkler, so lit up someone could use me to read by.

I opened my mouth . . . and . . . no. I couldn't do it.

Danielle and Moria looked at me curiously.

It was like some mutant alien had just snuck up and stolen my mojo.

Jupiter, I told myself sternly. *You can do this.*

I'd never sung in public alone like this. Should I juggle? What if no one even paused to watch? Was I great . . . or was I pathetic?

Epic fail!

I squatted by Edom. "Something's wrong," I whispered.

"Are you sure?" Edom asked. "Try again."

"No!" She was a great one to talk. "Maybe I can't do it without Orion."

Danielle blew softly into a tiny portable mic. "Hello, shoppers," she said. A few people smiled at her. "We're the Foodie Twins, and we love helping people figure out how to get kids to eat real food."

They definitely had mojo.

"We got our start at a farmers' market when our parents gave us money to buy something we hadn't eaten before," Moria said. "I picked out a kohlrabi because it made me think of a little spaceship. It's become one of our favorite vegetables."

People were slowing down to listen. "We like it raw," Danielle added. "Or you can grate it with apple and eat it with a cream dressing. The recipe is on our web page." She started passing out cards.

I bumped Moria's leg—or, rather, her spider-web tights. She was so close I could have bit her. "Excuse me," I said, getting up.

Oops. A guy with a farmers' market badge was standing by the entrance.

I hastily crouched back down.

Would the twins turn us in?

My heart went bounce bounce bounce.

"These kids are a good example," Moria continued. She leaned close to me and whispered, "Don't worry—Danielle and I have permission to operate here."

Yes! She was taking the busker high road.

Moria held the mic toward Edom. "What do you have in your wagon?"

Edom looked panicked.

"Raspberries," I said. At least I still had my speaking voice.

"Raspberries! Healthy choice! Yummy, too." Moria was giving us our opening. "If your kids plant something, they'll want to eat it," she told the crowd gathered around. "Did you plant these all by yourself?" she asked Edom.

"No." Edom pointed to me. "She helped."

People laughed as if Edom had made a good joke.

"Encourage these young foodies and entrepreneurs, ladies and gentlemen, and buy a raspberry plant," said Moria. "They're the future urban farmers of America."

From then on, I was busy figuring out change and saying thank-you-have-a-nice-day over and over until a woman with a big dog was suddenly asking, "You don't have any more?" Her dog pulled on its leash and tried to lick Edom's face.

I looked in the wagon. Seriously? Gone already? "Maybe next week." I pushed the dog away from Edom and it tried to lick my hand.

"Come on, girlfriend," the woman said to the dog. "You can't move in with them."

It made me miss Serena.

And that made me miss Orion.

"Block-walk," Danielle was saying to a man and woman near me. "It will only take about fifteen minutes away from your shopping, and you'll learn about food you can eat for free."

"Don't tell these hard-working vendors at the farmers' market," Moria added. She paused to adjust her pouch and refresh her sunscreen. "You and your sister should come along," she said to me. "You want to make money, right? I have a business proposition for you. It won't take long." She patted Edom's fluffy hair.

"She's not a mascot," I said. "Or a puppy." How many times and things did I have to explain, anyway?

"Sorry." Moria pulled her hand back quickly. She got down on Edom's level. "What's your name?"

"Edom." It came out squeaky but at least it came out.

"Like the cheese," Moria said. "Excellent."

The cheese? I couldn't remember any Tillamook sample like that.

She straightened up. "And you're Jupiter, right? Cool name. I like your beads."

Maybe these two weren't *so* awful. "I'll take our wagon to Mom and tell her we're going to join the block-walk," I told Edom.

This day might have opportunity knocking yet.

Chapter Twenty-Six

Ridin' on that New River train
Ridin' on that New River train
Same old train that brought me here
Is gonna take me back again.

Mom was looking dazed from the heat and the hard work of busking. "Your friends from last time," she said, squinting through the sweat. She gave them a little wave. "Sure—go on." She didn't even tell me to keep a good eye on Edom.

Either she was trusting me more or she was worn out and tired of worrying.

So before you could say "Whoa, Nellie," Edom and I were trotting past the umbrella-and-rooster sign with the block-walk group—six couples, and a guy with binoculars, and a gray-haired woman with a backpack. "We'll have you back in no time," Moria told everyone. We walked past the school and down the block. When we turned the corner, I saw houses with wind chimes on the porches and garden art in the yards.

Edom tugged my hand. "I *do* want to get to Amy-mom," she whispered.

I gave her a hard look. "You sure aren't acting like it."

"I do, though."

For some reason, I couldn't stay mad at her. "Okay," I said. "Moria and Danielle said they have an idea."

Moria was giving a spiel about foraging—how people had gathered food that way for centuries and how nature has lots of gifts if we take time and truly learn about them.

I'd spent plenty of time studying informal maps of abandoned fruit trees and other spots where delicious food was going to waste and no one cared if you helped yourself. Dad said never count on having someone around to feed you. "You and Orion are going to learn to be self-sufficient if it kills us," he'd say, laughing and rubbing the top of my head with his red beard.

"Uncle Max taught us all about eating wild plants," Moria said. "You can find them even in yards and alleys, but you have to do your research and know exactly what you're doing. Stick with someone like us until you're sure."

"We know this neighborhood inside and out," Danielle said. "Including which house owners don't use pesticides on their yards. Those are the only plants we'll eat. Uncle Max has survived for weeks only on what he can forage right in this Portland neighborhood."

Big deal. I'd foraged as a kid in a *forest*. I had a sudden memory of standing in a circle of ferns, looking up at Dad saying, "We need to figure out what to eat tonight."

He'd started to smile, and I could see he was going to tease me. "When you say 'we,'" he said, giving my ponytail a tug, "are you talking about you and a frog in your pocket?"

In my memory, I was standing there sort of laughing, sort of wanting to pat my pocket and . . . hungry. Good thing Topher had arrived later that afternoon with some supplies.

"Isn't it hard to get enough calories to live on?" I asked loudly.

Moria didn't get ruffled. "Yes. Especially in spring with no fruit, nuts, seeds, or roots available. Today, we'll show you things to tickle your taste buds."

Danielle displayed chickweed—the plant I'd been ripping out like stitches. "This plant is yummy, but near the end of its best season," she said. "Next to it is a common nuisance weed that the woman who owns this house is delighted to have us pick." She held it up. "Purslane. Try the stems and leaves in salads or sandwiches or any recipe that calls for spinach."

A woman clicked a photo. "Do you two really eat spinach?"

"Absolutely we do." Danielle nodded, sending her antennae dancing.

"The key is not to slime it up or cook it until it's stringy," Moria said.

Spinach? I thought. Is that all you've got? I couldn't

resist showing off a bit. "Isn't it possible to eat a weed and die?" I asked loudly.

Everyone turned my way. The geospace around me buzzed.

Danielle didn't flinch. "Absolutely!" she said. The faces swung back. "That's why we said you *have* to learn your stuff. Don't try this until you know completely what you're doing."

"Always use more than one of your five senses when identifying a plant you're going to eat," Moria said.

Danielle added, "For example, death camas looks like wild onion, but it doesn't have that oniony smell. If something tastes horrible, it probably isn't meant for humans to nibble on."

"We don't touch wild carrot," Moria said. They were like a Ping-Pong game. "Too many poisonous look-alikes. We'll show you only very safe plants today."

The group moved down the sidewalk. "Long ago," Danielle said, "humans counted on plants for food and medicine and lots of other things. When you forage, it connects you to something deep and real and old in yourself." She pulled a thermos and a glass jar from her

187

backpack and poured some water. "Your kids will think jewelweed is cool."

Moria held up a plant with a tiny orange flower. She picked a leaf and stuck it in the water. "See how it turns silvery?"

She held the glass up. The group clapped.

While Moria put the thermos away, Danielle said, "Later this summer, you can show your kids how to grab the seed pod tightly, and seeds will pop into their hands. They taste like teeny walnuts. Jewelweed can be made into ointment for scratches and bites, too."

As Danielle motioned for the group to follow her, Moria stopped Edom and me. "Your part is coming up," she said in a low voice. "One more stop and then we turn the corner and head for the grand finale."

"Why do you need us?" I asked.

"It's for our Uncle Max," Moria said. "He's been helping a friend with a cookbook. We promised we'd bring some new kid-volunteers."

"Volunteers for what, exactly?" I asked.

She didn't answer. "We also need an attention-getting photo," she said. "When I saw Edom, I knew she'd be perfect. She's so cute. I bet it'll go viral. People love cute stuff."

By now Danielle was a few yards away, showing off more plants. "I know she's cute," I said. "But what does she need to do?"

"Eat a bug."

"What?" I started to laugh. Edom who wouldn't even eat pepperoni?

"I'm serious," Moria said. "Insects are much more efficient than mammals at turning food into protein. You can help save the Earth. Danielle and I have done it—lots of times."

"Yeah?" I said. "Not going to happen."

I was going to miss having that money. But as Madam Marie would have said, it wasn't in the tea leaves. I'd have to think of something else to help with the grand plan.

Chapter Twenty-Seven

Come take up your hats, and away let us haste
To the Butterfly's Ball, and the Grasshopper's Feast.
The trumpeter Gad-fly, has summon'd the crew,
And the revels are now only waiting for you.
—*William Roscoe (1802)*

Moria launched into giving Edom and me a speech I could tell she had practiced—probably in front of a mirror. "Why should we think insects will taste icky?" She flung out one arm dramatically. "A grasshopper doesn't spend all its life underground the way a potato does. It hops from leaf to leaf soaking up the sun. Why wouldn't it taste like sunshine?"

Beside me, Edom shuddered as if she'd been asleep. Obviously, she'd been listening because she said, "It would burn your tongue."

I'd forgotten how literal she could be.

"Well—" Moria started.

"How much money?" Edom asked.

Seriously? I looked at her in admiration.

"Well—" Moria said again.

"And Jupiter has to do it, too," Edom said.

"Of course," Moria said. "That's what I meant. Both of you."

Ugh. But . . .

Moria let me squirm for a few seconds. The group was moving farther away. Behind us, a wind chime played a soft scale.

It *would* be a performance. People said if you fell off a horse, it was crucial to get right back on. "So you've eaten insects?" I asked.

"Naturally." Moria took a bow. "My favorite was cicada ice cream. Cicadas hardly eat anything the few days they're above ground, and they're full of vegetable goodness from tree roots."

"How much?" said Edom. When it came to money, she didn't get distracted.

"How about . . ." Moria paused.

"Are you sure you want to do it?" I asked Edom. How could insects possibly be Orthodox? She nodded. "Fifty-five bucks," I said before I could talk myself out of it.

"That's a lot," Moria said. "Uncle Max gave us a budget, and . . ."

Her words and face told me I wasn't seriously far off the mark. "Okay," I said to Edom. "We might as well head back to the farmers' market."

"Forty bucks," Moria said. "You'll see. It's not bad at all."

"Fifty-two. Final offer."

"Fifty."

"Deal," I said.

As we hurried to catch up with Danielle at the head of the tour, I tried not to think about fuzzy legs. Was this for really real? "It's still hard to believe you're—"

Danielle interrupted, impatient. "Because we're fraternal twins. We're not identical but we were born the same day. We've said that to 10,100 people."

Moria reached over and patted Edom's hair like she

couldn't help herself. "The date was March 15, the year of the rooster. We were born at the same time."

"In case you were wondering," Danielle added, "there is no year of the chicken. And I was born first."

"By, basically, two seconds," Moria said.

Danielle turned to the group. "At the corner," she called, "turn left. You'll see the food carts right away."

Food carts in the middle of a neighborhood?

Behind us, I could hear people starting to talk about their favorite food-cart treats. Wicked waffles. Grilled-chicken-and-coconut flatbread. Green-mango chutney. Samosas. Could there be an insect food cart? Tarantula mixed in with satay and momos? Instead of cookies made with dark chocolate and bacon, cookies made with dark chocolate and scorpion?

This whole thing was a joke.

Right?

But when we turned the corner, I spotted a lot, empty except for a few food carts. What really caught my attention, though, were the two long tables off to the side. Moria and Danielle headed right for them. Everyone followed.

I didn't dare look at Edom. My brain crackled—like when Orion and I were in the middle of an adventure that might be cool or might end in disaster. I could see a pile of cookbooks on one table. *Yum Bug: Saving the Earth While You Tickle Your Tastebuds.*

Uh-oh.

Behind the table was a guy wearing a chef's hat. *Uh-oh, uh-oh.* He welcomed the group and made a short speech about what a good source of protein bugs are.

A few new people wandered over to listen.

He held up a bowl. "Chex Mix tossed with crickets," he said. As we watched in a stunned kind of way, he grabbed a handful, chewed, and swallowed. "Don't collect food like this from an empty lot," he said. "You could take in small doses of pesticides."

More people stopped. Way more fascinating than carts with falafel or vegetarian torta.

"We're going to demonstrate just how do-able it is." The chef waved to Moria and Danielle. "If kids can do this, you definitely can too, right?"

Uh-oh. My electromagnetic field was buzzing to beat the band. I took Edom's hand. "Keep looking at me," I whispered. "Not at the crowd."

"I understand you have new volunteers for me," the chef said to Moria and Danielle.

They nodded and started clapping. People joined in. *Nooooo*, I thought. Then . . . *Money*, I thought.

I stepped forward.

"Keep your back to the group," I whispered to Edom. "Pretend they aren't there."

What would it be? Termites with crunchy wings? Roly-poly bugs?

The chef reached for a plate. I was definitely sweating.

"I've had people tell me that scorpion tastes like soft-shell crab," he told the group. "If I ask you how you think any bug will taste, most of you will say 'chicken,' but after people try a few I hear 'peanut butter' and 'citrusy.' The rest of the world thinks Americans are weird because we *don't* eat insects."

California dreaming . . . skateboarding . . . out on the paddleboard . . .

Mr. Bug Chef held something up. "Fried grass-hopper," he said.

I had a flash of Topher tapping two wood blocks together in a rhythm, saying, "Whales and birds are in love with melody, but bugs and frogs are in love with the beat."

No! Don't think about eating a fellow musician!

"Ready?" the chef asked.

Don't think about legs or wings, either. I gave Edom's hand a squeeze.

The audience hushed. According to Topher, when the chorus of frogs goes suddenly silent, it means danger is nearby.

I looked around.

Everyone was watching.

Well, I was a busker, wasn't I? *Orion, this one's for you.*

I opened my mouth. *Never let them see you . . .* The chef reached over. The second I felt something touch my tongue, the audience gave a satisfying gasp. I bit down.

Crunch.

It didn't taste like sunshine. Or chicken. Or peanut butter. Honestly, it didn't taste like much of anything.

But the texture would take some getting used to.

All the phones and pads and cameras aimed at me got my instincts going. I chewed and swallowed. The group clapped. I took a bow.

Wow. I'd eaten a grasshopper!

Now . . . I turned Edom slowly to face the audience and put my hands in front of her eyes. "Think about sunshine," I whispered in her ear.

"I'm thinking about Amy-mom," she whispered back.

"That's good, too."

At the last minute, I scrambled out of the way. Moria clicked the photo at exactly the right moment to catch Edom with a grasshopper leg sticking out the side of an enormous smile.

Chapter Twenty-Eight

The Marquam and the Fremont take the heaviest load.
They circle round the city in a ribbon of road.
On pilings of steel and concrete, they ride so high.
Night and day, the cars and trucks thunder along
Constantly singing a traveling song
While below the ships go sailing silently by.

Edom and I didn't stick around for any cookbook signing. Once Moria paid us, we ran back around the corner and down the street toward the farmers' market, laughing and high-fiving and fist-bumping.

"You were brave," I said to Edom. "Who knew you had a tough-girl routine deep down inside of you?"

"What's that?" She giggled.

"You'll see after you're here longer," I said. "Anyway, I'm positive now that you're ready for this

Greyhound trip. We can do it!"

"Really?"

"Really! And I'll bet we have almost enough money."

"Really?" Her face was shiny-bright with excitement.

"Let me show you how to do a chest bump." We practiced a few times until we were laughing hysterically. "Come with me to a post office," I said. "It'll only take a minute."

The woman behind the counter helped me look up the zip code for Longmont, Colorado. I bought a stamped postcard and put Dad's name and c/o General Delivery, like she told me to. I wished I could tell him that Madam Marie had seen Topher in tea leaves and now he was in Portland and what Mom had said in the car today and also about the freedom waiting for us right after the grand plan. But there wasn't room to write all that.

"Dear Dad," I wrote. "I really really need to talk to you. I have a phone now." I glanced around. What was Edom up to? She had something in a paper bag, but when she saw me looking she put it behind her back. I wrote down the phone number and signed my name.

Now I'd have to be sure to keep my phone with me all the time.

Even after we got back to the farmers' market, Edom kept her hands behind her back, which made her sort of waddle like a duck.

Victor was helping Mom load everything up. He wanted to hear all about the raspberries. "I hope Jess's grandmother is right and those little things will really grow," I told him.

"Oh, you can believe that gardener!" Victor put our wagon in and closed the back. "I saw a movie about a guy who had to grow food on Mars. If she'd been on that mission, she'd have had the whole place full of fruit and veggies and flowers."

All the way home, Edom and I kept looking at each other and giggling. Mom turned around with a puzzled expression. "Nothing," I said putting my hands out, palms up.

When Dad called, I'd tell him we were almost on the road again. For *staying* on the road, we needed Paddy Wagon. "Hey, Victor," I said. "Does it cost anything to hunt for sunstones?"

"Nah." He pulled up to our house. "As long as you want them for yourself. You can camp anywhere in the public collection area. Rabbit Basin has a pit toilet and picnic tables."

Hmmm. Not promising.

When we got to our room, Edom showed me what she had in the bag. A flat post-office box. "Free!" she said triumphantly. "I read it on the sign. Could we sell them?"

"No." I laughed. "Because anyone can get them free."

"Oh." She sagged and then brightened. "You could put your things in it."

"Edom," I said. "Bam! That's a great idea."

I counted out all the money and put my share—plus the rest of the Paddy Wagon fund and my other treasures—into the new box. When Edom pulled out her shoebox, she handed me a card. "Missing my beloved daughter on your beautiful and sad Gotcha Day," it said. "Stay well, my friend. I'll see you soon. Love Amy-mom."

"Was it weird when you heard you were coming to America?" I asked.

Edom looked mournful. "I was worried we'd never

go back to Ethiopia, and my grandma would be too sad. Why did Amy-mom have to get sick?"

"I don't know," I said. "What about your other mom. Were you . . . do you remember when . . ." I stopped.

Edom chewed on the sleeve of her sweater. "Amy-mom shows me lots of pictures. And takes me to see my grandma and helps me ask my grandma questions."

Edom's beeswax was some sad stuff. "What *do* you call the language your grandma speaks?" I asked.

"Amarinya." She gave me a tiny smile.

"Oh." I rolled the word around in my mouth. "I don't know if I'll remember how to say it, but I'll try." I couldn't take Edom all the way back to Ethiopia to see her grandma, but maybe it would help if she could go to the restaurant and hear that language and eat the right food.

That night, I was as bad as Edom, tossing and turning and wondering why Edom's birth mom had to die and Amy-mom *did* have to get sick, and thinking through the grand plan.

"Tell me the story again," Edom whispered.

I could do it without thinking: Number eight city bus. From the Steel Bridge we'd see the GO BY TRAIN sign. "Remember the boing-boing bridge?" I asked. "The Greyhound station is right there." I'd buy our tickets from a kiosk or find someone who would take us under her wing. Someone who'd understand about not patting Edom's hair and about eating Orthodox.

"What if somebody starts being scuzzbag to us?" Edom asked.

"Remember what to do?"

"Yes," she said. "If anyone offends me, I say, 'I need to go to the bathroom.' We'll lock the door and figure out what to do next."

"Good," I murmured. "And you remember if you see anyone in a uniform?"

As she took over telling the plan back to me, I must have drifted off because later I woke up and saw Edom drawing. The flashlight was propped on her pillow. "How come you draw elephants and roses anyway?" I asked sleepily.

"It's Amy-mom's getting-well room in her apartment." Edom showed me.

"I don't see Amy-mom."

"Because I can't draw people."

The night hung around us. "Oh," I said. "Did someone bring her roses?" Probably Topher. That guy was harder than a slug to get rid of. Madam said she'd tried beer, ammonia, diatomaceous earth, salt, copper barriers, oat bran, and ducks, and the slugs were still around. "What about the elephants?" I asked.

Edom's shadow head on the wall turned toward me. "My birth mom gave Amy-mom elephants every Christmas. Amy-mom put them on the shelf with the photo albums and we looked at them all the time."

"Carved elephants?" I asked and instantly thought, *Don't be ignorant.* Of course carved elephants.

"I put them under the roses in her room," Edom said. "So she would look at them every day and not forget."

"She's not going to forget you," I said.

"Tell me the story?" Edom asked.

I started all over again. "Remember where the city bus stops? Remember . . . look for an adult who's boarding and follow her so the bus driver won't think anything of it." On and on.

"What will you do after I'm in California?" Edom

asked. I was getting so tired that it was like her voice echoed through space.

"Come back here," I said. "Mom and Orion and I will spend the summer on the Oregon beaches." *Finally.* Yachats Fish Fry and the Celtic Music Festival and the Cape Perpetua Campground with the old trees that caught mist in their branches.

"Are you ever scared when you're on the road?" Edom asked.

"Of course not," I said. "After I get the lay of the land, nothing bad ever happens."

Only that one time.

That one time.

Under our beds, I could almost hear the dollar bills stirring—like earthworms—rustling their story that we could leave soon, soon, soon.

But did Edom have enough tough girl deep inside to sit alone with those elephants in the getting-well room?

I didn't need to think about that now. As the old song said, it would give me trouble in my mind.

Chapter Twenty-Nine

Where have you been, dear William, my son?
And where have you been, my darling young one?
I've been with my sweetheart; mother, make my bed soon,
For I'm sick at the heart and I now must lie down.

That week, Mom filled our living room with yellow and turquoise tiles that she'd picked up for the all-day job Cassandra set her up with. She kept trying different patterns. "I could really use Topher's painter's eye right now," she said. I looked at her sharply and she laughed as if she didn't mean it.

"Mom . . ." I sat beside her. She hadn't played the cello for days and days. "I know Dad isn't going to come back and live with us again. But do you think he'll visit?"

She hugged me. "I don't doubt the wind will blow that tumbleweed our way sometime."

"I sort of can't remember his face," I said.

She rocked me slightly back and forth. "Oh, Jupiter. Your dad had red hair and dark blue eyes. Nobody else ever had eyes that blue. Never forget how much he loves us."

For some reason, I wanted to hang my head and mournful cry. I did remember his beard. It was like a . . . well . . . like a wildfire. Once you saw a wildfire, you never got it out of your mind.

On Saturday, I made sure I had my phone, and we went to work. Madam Backyardigan set us to tidying the strawberry bed. The June-bearing plants were sending out masses of runners. "Snip them," she said. "Off they go."

Edom and I were both expert gardeners now. We snipped while orange and red daylilies waved around us like little campfires. "Did you ever go camping?" I asked Edom. "Did you ever eat s'mores?"

"I don't know what that is," she said.

I described our special s'mores the best I could, the crusty marshmallows, the thick Tony's Chocolonely chocolate bar, our favorite because we liked their slogan: "crazy about chocolate, serious about people." A flood of stars pouring across the sky. "Maybe you can go camping with us sometime," I said. "Mom and Orion and I will make our way down to California before the Oregon rains come."

Edom sat back on her heels. "If Amy-mom is . . ."

She didn't go on. I looked up and saw that her glasses were getting spotted. "Here," I said. "Don't cry." I rubbed them on a clean part of my shirt. "You know what?" The words came out before I could stop them. "If I put in my money from the Paddy Wagon fund we could go to California right now."

"Yes!" Edom jumped to her feet.

Why had I said that? My poor Paddy Wagon fund!

"Can we go tomorrow?" Edom asked.

"Tomorrow we're *skateboarding*."

"But this is important!" Edom stared down at me all bossy and confident.

A grasshopper has five eyes and they all look in different directions. That way, it doesn't have to keep turning its head to figure out if its prey is moving. I had the sudden sensation that I was prey to Edom. "You're not the only one in the universe, you know," I said. "I've been looking forward to skateboarding. And I *need* to fix Paddy Wagon."

"I already know about skateboarding!" She stomped her foot. "I already know about Paddy Wagon!"

My magnetic field—ten times stronger than the Earth's magnetic field—started buzzing bizarrely.

"Can we go day *after* tomorrow?" Edom asked. "On Monday?"

"Stop talking and let me think." I rubbed my head and went back to snipping runners. Greyhound probably had a morning bus. We could get on the road, and Mom would assume we had come over here to work as usual.

What was Madam going to think when she found out we'd deserted her yard? Would I ever come back and see it? If we did, would it be all choked with blackberries?

Ugh! Too sad! Back to the plan. Quick.

I knew Aunt Amy's address from the yellow envelopes. A city bus driver could tell us how to get to Balboa Hollow. After that, Topher could figure out what Edom needed. I patted my phone in my pocket.

If Dad called, I'd tell him everything.

He always had surprises up his sleeve. He could even walk up any minute.

Wait. Bad idea. Seeing me grubbing in the dirt wouldn't thrill him at all.

"Monday?" Edom asked again, like she'd stayed quiet as long as she could.

"Maybe," I said. "We'll make our final decision at the restaurant after skateboarding."

Someone at a place like that would be able to braid Edom's hair and talk to her. Maybe . . . even tell her it was a bad plan.

Did I want that?

It was hard to figure out *what* I wanted.

I was grouchy all day and even after we had eaten supper and gone to bed.

"Will you tell me the story?" Edom asked.

"No," I said. "I won't."

She curled up with her back to me, a small caterpillar in a cocoon. When that Greyhound bus arrived in San Francisco, she would be a butterfly and float free of me.

The thought made me feel flat and squirmy.

Chapter Thirty

Here I sit on Buttermilk Hill
Who could blame me, cry my fill
Every tear would turn a mill
Johnny's gone for a soldier

I woke up knowing sometime today I should tell Edom about that one time on the road that something seriously bad had happened. That way, she'd see how tough we needed to be every minute.

Not yet, though. I'd rather think about the day Mom unwrapped her shawl and that puppy peered out at us with curious eyes—head tipped, one ear up—and I practically couldn't see straight for love. Orion had stretched out his hands.

Mom handed the puppy to Orion. "What shall we call him?" It was as if the little dog was a big bar of lavender-scented soap that was washing Mom's world clean of everything that wasn't beautiful and soft.

I'd wanted so bad to hold him, but he was pawing at Orion's shirt as if he wouldn't be happy until he was right next to Orion's actual, beating heart.

Mom couldn't help but laugh, which made me start laughing, too.

"Traveler." Orion looked at us and his eyes were celestial. "Trav for short. Okay?"

"Sure," Mom said. "He was in a box in front of the 7-Eleven. Are you going to let your little sister hold him?" She practically had to pry Traveler away from Orion.

His fur was the color of my hair. I kissed his ear but I could tell that that dog was itching to get back to his star cluster.

From then on, Traveler and Orion were glued tight in a magnetic orbit.

Dad didn't feel the starlight from a four-legged traveler at all. "A dog?" He stared at Mom but she wouldn't meet his eyes. "What were you thinking? Pets weigh a family down. *Way* too much responsibility. Can't you take him back?"

Mom won that one, though.

Trav was the happiest, funniest dog ever. He ate carrots and bananas. That was when Orion and I started making the origami birds to draw in even more listeners and make better busking money. Also, Orion asked Topher to teach us tightrope skills. We practiced a *lot*. No idea too goofy when it came to getting money for buying dog food and avoiding hearing Dad say his favorite thing about Traveler: "That dog's been trouble since Day One."

Edom giggled in the living room, breaking the memory. Mom was laughing, too. I sighed, got up, and picked out a special floaty shirt. Time for serious planning about Monday. Food. Keeping our money safe. I got out my daypack and looked around the room.

It would be weird to not say good-bye to Madam or Victor or Jess.

How and when should I let Mom know where we were?

Jupiter, you can do this. Dad taught you to be self-sufficient and tough.

I dropped the pack on the floor and put my phone in my pocket.

Jess came to help Mom and Victor carry the tiles out to Victor's car. I waved good-bye as they pulled away. In the street, a black crow was pecking at a paper bag. "Those birds are like the guardians of the block," I said to Jess.

"You'll see something cool this fall," she said. "They drop nuts and wait for car tires to crack the shells."

In the fall we wouldn't be here.

Jess took us first to a tiny park with pavement and wildflowers—near the bus stop. "Your turn, newbie," she said. She showed Edom how to lie on the skateboard on her stomach and paddle along the sidewalk with her hands. As they practiced, I imagined myself shredding down a long hill, flying through time and space with my arms out, knees bent.

"Stop." Edom pointed. "Is that ladybug scat?"

Jess leaned over. "I think it's dirt." She wiggled the skateboard with her foot, making Edom giggle.

"Bugs don't wear diapers," Edom said, and giggled more.

"Baby goats make a lot of scat and you don't see them getting their diapers changed." Jess was laughing, too. "My grandma used to take me to see Portland city workers bringing goats to an empty lot to eat the weeds. She used to call me Goat Girl."

"Aren't you nervous to leave your grandma by herself?" I asked. "What about Public Enemy Number One?"

"Public Enemy Number One is my dad," Jess said. "He wants Grandma to move to assisted living. He said I could have one year living with her, and then she has to face the facts."

Even blessed thistle couldn't help some situations. "Hey," I said, "would you drop us off at an Ethiopian restaurant after skateboarding if I show you where it is?"

"I'll go with you," Jess said. "Now let's hit the big park. Follow me!"

Uh-oh. If Jess was with us at the restaurant, we couldn't discuss the plan.

A few blocks later, Prop—the pizza-maker from the

restaurant—was loading hiking gear into the back of a car, and he waved to me. His duffle bag said, GRAVITY KILLS. DEFY IT. I was ready to defy gravity. Jupiter ollieing over a garbage can, weightless and free.

"Do you like anything about elephants?" Edom asked Jess.

"I know that sounds random but she draws elephants a lot," I said.

"Sure," Jess said. "I like everything about elephants."

"Even their scat?"

I groaned.

"Especially their scat. Scientists have used elephant scat samples to help stop poachers. Whoa! Is that a turtle?"

Edom grabbed my hand.

"It's not scary," I said. "It would fit into one of Madam's big pots. Do you want to touch it?"

Edom tried to pull me back. "Don't even pet Victor's chickens unless you ask first," she said.

"Hey, Ms. Evangel," Jess called. "Did you know anything about this turtle?"

Ms. Evangel stopped clipping her hedge. "It

belongs to that young man next door. He says it doesn't bite. But I'm not getting my fingers anywhere near it."

Jess hopped onto the porch next door and knocked.

"You're knocking like a white girl," Ms. Evangel called.

"I am a white girl." But Jess went *bam bam* with her fist and even gave the door a kick.

The door opened and a man with a blond ponytail stuck his head out.

"Is this yours?" Jess pointed to the turtle.

"Hey thanks." He came out. "I keep trying to find a place for him to get fresh air, but he's an escape artist."

"That's one ugly escape artist," said Ms. Evangel as Jess came back toward us. "Guess it's craving Independence Day." She picked up a red, white, and blue hat and put it onto the head of her dog statue. "Happy birthday to America."

"Were you born in this land?" Edom asked.

"Emmanuel Hospital, right down that way." Ms. Evangel gestured vaguely.

"Were you?" Edom asked Jess.

"Yep." She waved good-bye to Ms. Evangel and started off.

"Was everybody but me?" Edom stuck to Jess's side, looking up at her—very earnest. "My body is America on the outside," she said, "and Ethiopia on the inside."

I felt sort of alien, myself, today.

"Park right ahead," Jess said. "And look! A bee! A pollinator, deliciously alive."

"Big deal," I said. "A bee." I could hear sounds of kids screaming and playing. Too bad we were on our way out of Portland before we discovered this park so close to the house.

"It is a big deal," she said. "Who's going to save them if we don't?"

I didn't know who was going to save them, but right now, I had one thing and only one thing on my mind: *Live to skate, skate to live.*

Showtime.

Chapter Thirty-One

I remember one evening in the pouring rain
And in my heart was an aching pain
Fare thee well, O Honey, fare thee well.

We followed the noise of screaming and laughing kids through the park and ended up at a playground—and right there was a paved area with a freestanding ramp. I stretched out and took deep diaphragm breaths like when Orion and I were preparing to sing.

"Too crowded," Edom said, refusing to look at the swings and monkey bars.

"There's a fountain by the rose garden." Jess pointed. "We'll go there next."

"Now," Edom said. She had on her stubborn clam look.

"No!" I said. This was my time, not hers. I can take you to the fountain tomorrow, I started to add, but I caught myself. Was it really, truly possible that tomorrow we could be gone?

Of course it was possible. I could do it!

Concentrate, I told myself. *You are confident and bold*—and skateboarding was just the thing to make me *feel* it. Good thing I had chosen such a floaty, dramatic shirt. Also, good that no real skate rats were using the ramp today.

"Look!" Jess said. "More bees. This, my friends, calls for a celebration. The dudettes that dance with the flowers." The tattooed wings danced on her shoulders.

What a one-track pollinator mind! I checked for pinecones or rocks. Put my foot on the board and tilted it. It was time to flow with the go, as skaters said.

Jess took elbow and knee pads and a helmet from her backpack. Edom slumped against a big rock near where kids were pushing each other on a little merry-go-round, making everyone's hair whip around as they flew. "I don't like this park," she said.

"Chill, Edom." I put on the safety equipment, and Jess adjusted the helmet straps. When I was ready to roll, I shuffled my feet to feel the grippiness of Jess's board.

Everyone falls, Orion told me the first time. Then they fall harder. That summer I had scabs everywhere. But being willing to see a little blood makes you a skater.

I shoved off. *Keep most of your weight on the deck.* For a second, it felt weird to be going sideways. Then things started coming back. In my mind, Orion and I were tick-tacking along a sidewalk beside a snoozing tiger made of sand. If you're going to busk, you have to get people's attention, and sometimes that means you have to be more interesting than beach art, so you can't obsess about having too much dignity.

I picked up speed—with a quick glance back.

Jess was talking to some adults. Probably about bees. I was wrong that she was like me. She was a rescuer of bees and turtles . . . and grandmas. I'd have to warn Edom not to even hint about our plan in front of Jess.

She'd say it was a rotten idea.

And maybe it was.

I ambled toward the ramp—and away. Take it easy, I thought. Don't push too fast.

Now Edom was hugging her knees and looking miserable. A kid was doing wheelies around her but not in a hassling way. Still, I felt my heart twist.

Concentrate, Jupiter.

In California, I'd landed two 180 pop-shoves and after about three months, I could do a real ollie. Now, two kids riding on one bike went up the ramp and dropped off. The guy on the back gave me a grin.

Big deal. I was almost ready, myself.

Who was going to help Edom in California? Kids in school were going to think her fluffy hair looked cute to touch. Someone was going to tease her for having a cheese name.

Concentrate.

"It's time to go to the restaurant," Edom yelled.

"Pretty soon," I yelled back. I tick-tacked toward Edom and flashed her a peace sign.

She shook her head. "I. Want. To. Go. Now."

"Hang on. I barely got started."

I sped up, feeling my shirt flutter. "That your sister?" the guy pedaling the bike called.

Today wasn't for thinking about explanations or Edom or bees with their amazing superpowers. It was time for something glittery. Maybe someone would holler, "Sick trick!"

I heard footsteps behind me and did a quick check over my shoulder. Edom. "Cool it!"

She lunged like she was going to grab me. "The restaurant. You promised."

"Stop that!" I pushed off hard with my left foot.

"Wait!" she yelled.

I didn't wait. I soared away, gathering speed, and came around in a circle again—zooming toward Edom who was right in my path. Ha! Big, bold Jupiter. Rock the fakie.

With a little wiggle, I dodged around Edom.

Her hand was on my shirttail and before I could react, I felt the yank.

My feet flew off the board.

Whomp!

I crashed to the ground smack on my butt.

Ouch! The pain jolted through me like a thousand slamming meteors.

"Sorry!" Edom was leaning over me. "Are you all right?"

Tornadoes on the Red Spot of Jupiter! "No!" I hollered. "Forget the plan! Forget you! Forget everything! You've been nothing but trouble since Day One!"

Chapter Thirty-Two

Oh the times they are hard
And the wages they are low.
Close your eyes, my dear
So you will not see me go.
Listen to the whistle blow
A hundred miles.

Edom took off on a full-pelt run with Jess hustling after her.

After a minute, I wobbled to my feet and took off my helmet. "You okay?" the guy on the front of the bike called. The other kid hopped off the back and retrieved Jess's board for me.

"Yeah," I said. Grumpy and hurt.

Forget Edom! I kicked a stick and sent it spinning. I felt like killing something. A slug would be perfect.

A plop of water dropped on my face, and then another and another. Chilling me out. Then the rain quit like it couldn't be bothered. Jupiter has the scariest atmosphere in the Milky Way—because of its radiation belt. I guess I looked pretty scary to Edom.

I picked up the skateboard, rubbing my aching backside. Who knew someone as little as an ant compared to me could confuse me so much? When Jess asked me what had happened, I would say, "I know Edom seems harmless and even cute. But you don't have to share a room with her."

I started walking away.

Why did people have to cause so much trouble?

As I limped out of the park, I thought about Mom, all achy with playing the cello and laying tile. Probably she didn't start out thinking this Edom gig was going to be that hard. Orion and I sometimes sang a song, "I've been with my sweetheart; mother, make my bed soon, for I'm sick at the heart and I now must lie down." You think the poor guy has a stomachache. Then . . . *wham*. You realize his sweetheart has poisoned him and he's going to die.

Letting people get too close was what led to songs of sorrow and desolation. As Dad said, the only way to keep the sadness off was to keep moving.

Jess came trotting toward me. "Are you okay?" she asked.

"I guess." I handed the skateboard and her other stuff to her.

"When I turned thirteen and was mad at everyone," Jess said, "my grandma let me plant things with gruesome names like Love Lies Bleeding, and Love in a Mist, and Bloody Fingers."

It must be pretty great sometimes—having a grandma. "How's Edom?" I asked.

"She'll be fine. The van is coming to take Grandma to physical therapy, and I told Edom to wait with her while I retrieved you. Edom's sure you won't go to the Ethiopian restaurant, now, but I told her you probably would."

"Yeah," I said. "Even though I'm still pretty annoyed with her."

I limped along. When we got to the mossy oak tree, I heard someone singing a bluesy song. The notes hung there like they would pull down the sky.

I picked up a stick and drummed garbage and recycling bins all the way down our block.

"Do you think . . ." I stopped.

"Wait," I said. "The front door is open. Didn't you say you sent her out back?"

Jess and I hurried up the steps and into the house.

Edom's shoebox and my box were sitting in the middle of the bedroom and I knew instantly what was going on.

Chapter Thirty-Three

It was late last night, when my lord came home
Inquiring for his lady, O!
The servants said on every hand,
"She's gone with the raggle-taggle gypsies, O!"

"What?" Jess looked from the empty boxes to me. "What?"

"I think she went to the Greyhound station," I said. The doll was gone. And my daypack.

"The *Greyhound* station?" Jess headed for the living room with me on her heels. "Fuzz it! You're joking, right?"

"No," I said. "Because—"

"Never mind." She looked around frantically. "We've got to find her. I'll see if Victor can drive us."

In my mind I saw that guy with the black beard . . .
blocking Edom on the sidewalk . . . grabbing her shoulder.

I knelt on the floor, trying to hold in my exploding
thoughts. Bees buzzed in my brain—and not Jess's bees.
Angry, mean ones. Terrifying ones.

I'd never felt this scared. Except . . .

The awful memories bombarded me like terrible
flying debris.

Crackling yellow and orange flames—a wildfire tearing
up the California grass.

Smoke like dragon's breath hot, hot into my chest.

And Traveler.

He loved barreling down the slope and leaping into
the water where Dad was concentrating on getting us
things to eat. Finally, Dad yelled at Orion, "Would you
keep him away so he doesn't scare away the fish. That
dog's been nothing but trouble since Day One."

Orion had argued but it hadn't done any good.
When Dad was gone, Orion and Trav had headed off
for a long walk.

I was tossing pebbles in the stream by the camp

when I spotted smoke in the gorge.

"Orion!" I hollered as loud as I could. "Mom! Come quick!"

A few minutes later, I heard my brother running. "Stay!" he shouted at Traveler as he crashed through the water toward me. "Get our stuff into Paddy Wagon!"

Flames came charging up the valley and into the campsite. I never knew fire could run, and I mean run, like on yellow and red legs.

Now as I knelt in the Portland living room, a plane roared overhead and my memories came back in bursts.

Mom racing toward us with her guitar banging and bouncing against her leg.

Orion trying to protect our stuff, beating at the flames with wet towels and T-shirts and anything he could grab.

Trav standing on the rocks, barking.

Me. Running. Yelling. "Dad, dad, dad, dad, dadadadadadadadad!"

Mom catching up and grabbing me from behind

and hauling me back, kicking, up the steps and into Paddy Wagon. "Stay there!" she shouted. Fierce.

I was on her heels—right back out on the steps. She had had time to give me one blistering glance before she got to Orion. And then Dad was back, panting and sucking breath in.

"Help them!" I screamed.

Dad dropped the fishing pole. Next thing I knew he was wrestling Orion toward the van. Orion shouting, "Wait! Stop!"

Me hanging on Dad's arm shouting, "Dad! No!"

Dad lifted us both into the van and held Orion from grabbing the door handle. "Go!" he shouted. Mom peeled rubber through the charcoal grass. I stumbled to a window to look back.

You couldn't even see the stream because of the flames.

Oh, Traveler.

When Orion stopped fighting and dropped down to the floor he was coughing and choking black stuff out of his nose. "Take me back," he whispered. "Take me back."

"I'm not endangering my family for a dog," Dad said.

I crawled over and tried to put my whole self around Orion. Even if my skinny arms had been made of iron, I wouldn't have been able to make him feel them.

We stopped for the night in the nearest town. I don't think Orion slept at all. As soon as the sky was ashy light, Mom drove us back to the campsite, but no matter how long we whistled and called, we never found a trace of Traveler. "Anything worth its salt can survive out here until the next hiker comes along," Dad said. "A family like ours has no business with a dog."

I held it together until two days later when we were in a café and Topher walked up to the table. "Hey, Orion and Jupiter," he said. Orion just kept pushing his eggs around the plate, but I dropped my glass, and orange juice spilled everywhere, and Topher pulled me onto his lap and rocked me back and forth and didn't care that I got him all sticky.

Suddenly I heard Jess on the porch.

"Couldn't find Victor," she called as she pushed the door open. She had her phone out. "Must be on his motorcycle, but I don't care. I'm texting him."

I felt dizzy with fear.

"Victor gave me his number when Grandma moved back," Jess said. "He's a good guy. If he hears his phone, he'll pull over and check it out." She ran one hand through her hair.

Think, Jupiter, think.

Mom wouldn't be back for hours. Planet Jupiter, all alone in the universe.

"Maybe we should call the police," Jess said. "Although we'd have to wait for the officer to get here . . ."

"She'll hide if she sees someone in uniform," I said. Like I'd coached her to.

Jess frowned. "Okay. But if we don't catch up with her in the next twenty minutes, I'm definitely doing it. I'll run over and see if Grandma might still be there."

As soon as she was gone, I put my hand into my pocket and touched my phone.

Don't call, I told myself.

Don't call.

Don't call—

Chapter Thirty-Four

Last night you slept on a goose feather bed,
With the sheet turned down so bravely, O!
Tonight you'll sleep in a cold open field,
Along with the raggle-taggle gypsies, O!

I called.

Topher answered immediately.

"I need you," I said. "Bad."

"Be right there," he said. That's what he used to say when Dad or Mom called him to rescue us.

Jess shoved through the door. "I saw the van driving off." She was panting. "Grandma waved to me out the window like she didn't have a care in the world."

"Got . . . someone," I told her. "He'll be right here."

"Okay." She started pacing. "Now why the Greyhound station, of all sketchy places?"

I filled her in as much as I could as fast as I could. "I screwed up big time," I said. "You don't have to come if you don't want to."

"*I* screwed up big time! I was the one in charge." Jess stopped pacing. "Edom knows where to catch the city bus? I'll run over there."

As soon as she was gone, I grabbed a piece of paper and tried to write something for Mom, but what? How was I going to tell her that I lost Edom?

Mom was never going to forgive me.

Hold it together, Jupiter—planet of ice and rock. I'd given Edom survival skills. *Look bold and like you know what you're doing. Always locate the nearest rest room or other safe place. Go there if you see someone in uniform who might stop you. Pretend you're with an adult. Keep your things close to your body.* Even birds and caterpillars know how to fool predators.

Maybe she never made it onto the city bus. Maybe . . .

Jess came running back around the corner.

Alone.

I hugged my stomach to press the panic out. Why hadn't the crows—guardians of the street—called out? Flapped their wings in her face?

Hold it together, Jupiter.

"Does she have her doll with her?" Jess asked. "Thinking of things to say if we *do* need to call the police."

"Yes." Edom and that pathetic doll walking along with a police person looming over her. Did I even teach her our address?

Topher's car came around the corner, and I jumped up.

That car. So many times to the rescue but this time was different.

"You're a friend of a family?" Jess asked as Topher swung himself out of the car. His hair was falling down over his black glasses. I used to pinch it back with one of my barrettes when we read together.

He nodded to Jess but looked at me. Serious. Worried. "Hey, Green Bean. Where's your mom?"

I glared at him. *Hold it together, Jupiter.* My feet started toward the car.

"She's on a job," Jess said in a high, scared voice.

"We don't know where. Thanks for coming for us. Jupiter says Edom went to the Greyhound station by herself and—"

"You never should have brought Edom to Oregon!" The words burst out of my mouth.

Jess glanced at me. "I'll get in front," she said to Topher. "Fill you in as we drive. Just hurry, okay?"

I yanked the back door open and ducked into the seat, managing to hit my head. *Blam.*

"Mom and me . . . we aren't any good at taking care of a kid," I said, buckling up. Groaning. "You know we're buskers, not babysitters."

Topher pulled away from the curb. "Greyhound station? Wow, that's . . . how did she . . ."

I pressed my hand against my hurting head. "Yes, Greyhound station. And she went by city bus like I taught her to do. Please stop asking questions and just go. Fast."

The oak tree went by. The coffee shop. Jess filled Topher in.

"I'll bet city bus drivers are good at spotting lost kids and knowing what to do," Topher said, tipping the rearview mirror down so he could see me.

I refused to catch his eye. Not this kid—I'd taught her too well.

Topher steered down the ramp onto I-5, but it didn't take two minutes before traffic pooled up in a dam, slowing us down to a crawl.

Oh, Edom.

I couldn't breathe. This car didn't have enough air in it.

"Have you called the police?" Topher asked. He drummed nervously on the wheel. I had an odd, random memory of sitting with Topher and Orion and Trav, surrounded by huge smooth river stones, coaxing out soft drum sounds with our fingers while the dog tipped his head to listen.

"Not yet," I said. "Police will just scare her and make her hide." What if they took Edom away from us? Police usually weren't fans of buskers and families like ours.

"I haven't been driving in Portland that long," Topher said to Jess. "Would it be quicker to exit?"

"We gotta get across the river somehow." Jess sounded like the air was too thin for her, too. "I think the jam will loosen up right after this. She knows where to get off the city bus?" she asked me.

"Pretty sure," I said. Images filled my mind: That first day with the rental car. Our trip to the boing-boing bridge. I'd give anything to be back then. Helping a guy in a wheelchair fill up his water bottles at the fountain. Edom and me splashing each other. Running around squealing.

We sat in silence for a few minutes. Jess tried Victor's number two more times and left a message that Victor should get Mom and come to the Greyhound station and that it was urgent.

If we didn't find her . . .

Please be right there inside the station, Edom.

"How do you fit into things?" Topher asked Jess.

"I was babysitting today. I live next door—for a year so my grandma could stay in her home. Now . . ." Jess didn't finish because the traffic jam suddenly broke and we were moving and she was taking quick, shallow breaths and looking out the window.

Topher exited I-5 and the Broadway Bridge was coming toward us and—seconds later—we were out over the wide water and I saw the sign: GO BY TRAIN.

Edom.

The way her glasses made her eyes big and superscared. "Can you check on your phone when the Greyhound bus leaves for California?" I asked Jess.

Go. Go. Go. We got to the end of the bridge. Swung into the left turn lane.

Jess looked up. "Six twenty-five p.m."

So she wasn't on her way to California yet. *Be there! Be right inside the Greyhound station doors.* Topher turned left again. I saw the sign with the long, running dog: CUSTOMER PARKING. Jess pointed at it.

I rubbed hard on Topher's dusty car window. There. The tower of piled-up stones near the bus station. Mom said the sculptor wanted to remind travelers about cairns that show hikers the path in the wilderness. This one looked like it was about to topple.

Like me.

Topher parked, and the three of us scrambled out and ran down the brick sidewalk past sleeping bags and a woman leaning on a shopping cart.

Please be there. Please be right there.

The automatic doors opened too slowly. I dashed in and saw that the station was huge—a long narrow room. A couple of people were lined up where a sign said Information and Tickets. A few more were scattered around sitting and looking at their devices.

No Edom.

I looked around frantically.

"Someone should have spotted her." Topher headed to a guy wearing an official-looking vest.

Jess started in the opposite direction toward Information and Tickets. I knew Edom better than either one of them did. She had skills—thanks to me.

Get the lay of the land, Jupiter.

Lockers? Too small for her to fit into. Souvenir shop? It was easy to duck in, duck out.

But no Edom.

Hurry. Hurry.

I glanced at Jess. The woman behind the counter was shaking her head.

Snack bar? I ran that way.

No. Nobody buying food. Go on into the room with big tables?

Instead, I turned around and looked at the roped-off area. TICKETED PASSENGERS ONLY BEYOND THIS POINT. But Edom could have followed a family or slipped in when no one was looking.

A television blared. An announcer talking, all serious and full of doom. Something bad was happening somewhere.

She might have gotten off the bus and walked the wrong way. She could be anywhere in this enormous city. Where rogue planets wandered starless.

Jess had turned away from the information counter and was moving at a run toward places I'd already checked out. Topher was talking to someone on a bench. I tried to put myself into Edom's brain.

Did she forget everything she knew? When she freaked, she usually froze . . . she . . .

Wait.

Locate your safe place.

Oh.

Chapter Thirty-Five

The water is wide, I cannot get o'er
And neither have I wings to fly
Build me a boat that can carry two
And both shall row, my love and I.

I stared at the roped-off area. A handwritten cardboard sign had been added below the TICKETED PASSENGERS ONLY sign: NO BATHROOM ACCESS. I waited a few agonizing seconds for the guy with the vest to turn his back.

Two hundred billion stars in the Milky Way and this one measly moon.

There. The security guy looked away. I slipped under the barrier and crossed the room quickly and quietly toward the blue sign: WOMEN DAMAS.

I ducked inside. White tile everywhere. Someone changing a diaper at the pull-down table. A woman in shorts standing by a sink brushing her teeth.

I went right, then left—checked out two rows of stalls.

No Edom.

"Did you see a little kid come in here?" I asked.

Both women shook their heads no. The one at the changing table looked like a grandma. She'd be smart and experienced, but that toddler on the table took all her attention.

The other woman was young.

I leaned against a wall feeling dizzy and trying to slow my shallow breathing. I'd been so sure she'd be in here.

Drip.

Drip.

Drip.

"Come on," the diaper-changing woman said. "Up you go." She headed out. The toddler stared at me over her shoulder.

The other woman spit and splashed water. *Calm,*

Jupiter. Get the lay of the land. I looked around again. One stall door was shut.

I tried to peek in through the gap where the door closes and then bent over and looked under.

No shoes.

I pushed gently but the door didn't give. "Edom?" I called over the loud *whoosh* of the dryer.

No answer. I felt pretty foolish speaking to a door. But Edom *had* to be in there, didn't she? Following everything I'd taught her, exactly? The young woman was watching me in the mirror. "Are you sure," I asked her, "that you didn't see—"

Before I could finish, she shook her head again.

The stall could be locked because the toilet was broken. Still . . . "I don't care that you took the money," I said to the door. "Not one bit."

The woman gave me a quick glance and then hurried out. Would she call security? The room felt horrifyingly empty.

Should I stick my whole head under that small gap, no matter how rude that made me? Grab the door? Rattle it ferociously?

My heart was beating a terrible, hard rhythm. "Edom," I said. "I know you're there!"

Was that a sound? A creak from shoes standing on a toilet seat? I put my ear against the door.

Think, Jupiter.

With my inner eye, I saw Edom on that first day. Braids and beads—with Bach soaring and filling up the room.

I gave the door a kick. How could I get her to open it? She could be so stubborn.

She could be so scared.

How could I get her out?

Could I somehow do what Mom did using horsehair and goat guts?

Impossible.

Or . . . not?

"The water is wide," I sang—or sort of croaked. "I cannot get o'er." Could I sync Edom's heartbeat to me? I took a quick breath and kept going. "And neither have I wings to fly." I felt like I was choking. But I did everything I could to fill the echoey room with the cello's tenderness. "Build me a boat that can carry two, and both shall row . . ."

Someone's feet hit the floor.

I thought I would cry and hug her. But that's not what happened at all.

Chapter Thirty-Six

Fare thee well, cold winter,
and fare thee well cold frost.
Nothing have I gained,
but a sister I have lost
Sailing down the winding river
I must go.

Jupiter spinning.

You can't even tell what it is about that kid who is looking at you with her scared eyes in the white bathroom tile glare that makes you so mad.

You grab her arm so hard you know it hurts. She says "ouch" but you don't let go. "I only spent one-twenty-five of your money," she says. "The rest is right there. In the bag."

"So what!" you shout. "What you did wasn't safe!"

The loud voice bounces off of sinks and mirrors. A thought filters through the atmosphere. *You were terrified for her.*

"Why should you care?" she shouts back.

"I don't care!"

The instant those rock-snot words flew out of my mouth, the spinning stopped. I let go of Edom's arm and leaned my forehead against a sink, catching my breath.

Drip.

Drip.

"Of course I care," I said. "You're my cousin. Practically my sister."

She rocked her doll silently.

I straightened. Took a deep breath.

I went over and got down and put my arms around her and squeezed as hard as I could.

"You're squishing me!" she said.

"I'm proud of you," I said. "You did a great job with using your noodle."

She almost gave me a tiny smile.

"We made a good plan," I said. "But it was way too big for us. Topher is here and I *promise* he'll help figure out how to get you back to Amy-mom."

Now she let me take her hand. I picked up the daypack and led her out of the bathroom.

"There they are!" Jess shouted.

She and Topher were rushing toward us. We met at the NO BATHROOM ACCESS sign with everyone grabbing everyone as if we were hanging on for dear life. Suddenly I saw Mom coming through the door of the Greyhound station, her face all terrified. Edom ran. Mom opened her arms and dropped to her knees on the dirty floor.

Then I was running, too, and Edom wrapped herself around Mom, and I was only a few steps behind, and Mom was reaching out with one hand, and I was falling into the gravitational pull of Planet Mom.

"I'm sorry," I mumbled.

"No, I'm so sorry." She said the words into my neck. "I thought I could do everything but I can't. I'll figure out something different. Everything has *got* to be different."

After long minutes, she let us go and stood up. "Thank you," she said to Topher and threw her arms around him. For a second, he looked surprised. Then they rocked back and forth, while Edom hung onto Topher's knees.

I sensed Jess watching me—and I was right. "What?" I asked.

"Just checking to see if you're cool." She was half smiling, trying not to crack a full grin.

I picked up Edom's bag from the floor. "Why wouldn't I be cool? So they love each other. So big deal." Victor hurried through the doors, right then, so I hugged him, too, and the whole group of us walked through the staring people—who weren't even pretending not to stare—and out into the bright sunshine.

When we got to the parking lot, there was an awkward moment of everyone looking at everyone else. Different? What did that actually mean? And that hug? Was I *really* okay with this annoying thing between Mom and Topher?

Edom was chewing on her sweater sleeve and I remembered my promise. "Is it okay if I ride with Topher?" I asked Mom.

"Jupiter!" Mom sounded shocked. "I have no idea what's really going on, and you're running off again already?" I could tell she was kind of joking and kind of not.

"I know," I said. "But I promised Edom something. Something Topher needs to help figure out."

"Can't I help?"

"Mom." I gave her a big squeeze. "I promise I'll tell you everything as soon as I'm home. But . . . Topher . . . well . . . All for one, and one for all, you know."

She probably never thought she would hear those words coming out of *my* mouth.

Topher nodded at Mom. "It'll give me a chance to show Jupiter and Edom a piece of art I've been working on."

Mom thought for a minute and then nodded slowly. "I guess it isn't going to be that easy to know how to do *different*," she said.

"But we have a good team," I said, giving Jess and Victor a little thank-you wave. And if Topher wasn't on the team, I didn't know who was.

"Can I come with you?" Edom was holding onto Topher's pocket.

It was her life we were talking about. "I want you to come," I said.

Mom sighed. "All right, cowboy," she said to Topher.

"But do not let them out of your sight." She kissed her fingers and touched my cheek. "I'll get supper together," she said. "See you at home soon."

As Topher and Edom and I were driving over the Broadway Bridge, I kept hearing Mom's voice saying, "Everything has *got* to be different." Those words felt scary—but *different* also meant much more breathing room in this car now that we weren't afraid that Edom was whirling through space like some celestial dust bunny.

Topher cleared his throat.

Whatever was coming out of his mouth next, I wasn't ready. "Would you roll the windows down?" I asked.

"Sure."

He was always so good about *take your time.* I needed to explain about how much Edom wanted to get back to Amy-mom—and how he was the logical person to drive her there and figure everything out and maybe even stay with her. . . . Not yet, though. Not for a few minutes.

Edom and I turned toward the breeze. "Your doll probably wants wind in her face, too," I said to Edom. "What's that doll's name, anyway?"

Edom gave me a tiny smile. "Enku." She held the doll up to the window and whispered to her.

I yawned.

Topher caught my eye. "It sure has been a tough day, right?"

"Yeah," I said. "But also Edom doesn't believe in sleep. I don't know why."

"It's personal," Edom said.

Seriously? We were back to that again?

I'd better figure out how to show her I was serious about my promise. "Were you surprised when Aunt Amy showed up in San Francisco after all these years?" I asked Topher.

"A little." He smiled at me. "When our garage band broke up, I lost touch. But, you know, Facebook came along . . . and there was Amy all the way from Ethiopia! I liked reading her posts about everything she was doing."

We got off the freeway into a neighborhood of nice-looking houses and old trees. Topher stopped for a red light, and I hugged my elbows, trying to think what to say next.

"I know it was hard for you when I left," Topher said, looking at me in the mirror again.

"It was *fine*," I said. Then I stopped. "Or, technically, no. No, it wasn't."

"It was hard for me, too," he said, very seriously. "I couldn't think what to do next, so I wandered around the Newport aquarium and watched the octopus. Smart creatures."

He and I had spent so many hours waiting for that shy guy to emerge and show itself to us. "An octopus can screw the top off a jar," I said. "It can trick its prey by tapping it on the shoulder and making it look the wrong way."

"Yep," Topher said. "And it has three hearts."

"I know," I said.

How could a three-hearted octopus stand all those feelings?

When Topher paused for a left-hand turn, I stared out at mossy trees linking branches over Klickitat Street.

"I saw your mom the day before I drove up here," Topher said to Edom. "She's almost well enough to be with you again."

Edom made a small, scared sound. "Is she making plans without me? Is she thinking about never going back to Ethiopia?" Topher started to say something, but Edom rushed on. "Or is she going home to Ethiopia and leaving me here? Because I won't be so much trouble on the trip this time. Jupiter taught me lots of things about using my noodle."

I could hardly bear to look at her. How many things had she been worrying about?

"Remember when I came to stay with you the first night she had to be in the hospital?" Topher asked.

Edom leaned forward as far as the seatbelt would let her.

"We were drinking cocoa and you told me, 'She'll come back. She's my forever family. A forever family means even if you try to get them off of you, they're stuck to you.'"

That's the part Dad hated, I thought. He and I used to sing the I-don't-need-nobody songs.

"Amy isn't the sort of person who would ever willingly leave you in the lurch," Topher said. "She sent you to Oregon because it was an emergency. But she can't wait to sit with you and talk about plans for after she's all strong again." He slowed down and put his blinker on. "Almost there," he said.

For some reason, as we drove the last few blocks, all I could think about was the time Mom and Orion and Topher and I spent the evening throwing Mom's collection of sea glass toward the moon. "When the moon was young," Topher had said that night, "it was 14,000 miles away. Now it's more than 238,000 miles, moving a little farther all the time."

Like Dad.

I'd cried. A little. But when Topher shined a flashlight into a tide pool and helped me touch the sticky fingers of a sea anemone, I quit. That night, Mom and Topher sang us to sleep with Dad's favorite songs.

"There's the house where I've been staying," Topher said. "The yellow one."

That night, Dad left us in the lurch.

Amy wasn't that kind of person. Neither was Mom or Topher or Orion.

I didn't want to be that kind of person either.

Topher parked and came around to open the doors.

Maybe I was going to be mad at Dad for a while, and maybe he'd be mad at me, too, because I wanted an orbit again, even with gravity holding things in place and everything. Maybe I liked the feeling of having a forever family. So what? "I just wanna say that any trouble you brought into my life was no big deal," I told Edom. "I'm going to miss you."

"I'm going to miss you, too," she said.

Thinking about the black hole she was going to leave behind when she went to California scooped my center right out.

Chapter Thirty-Seven

Oh my darling, oh my darling
Oh my darling, Clementine.
You are lost and gone forever.
Dreadful sorry, Clementine.

Topher's masterpiece—which was painted on a garage—was an enormous elephant that looked at people on the sidewalk with stern, wise eyes. Its ears fanned wide and its tusks were majestic.

The elephant.

The myth.

The legend.

In the painted sky over its head, the universe swirled. Edom and I stared up at the solar system, which is full of planets and moons and comets and asteroids and minor planets and dust and gas—but where sadness can get you even when you're out in the middle of two billion stars.

I saw Orion's belt—those three bright stars. Dad's face was painted on a comet. Mom and Topher were both gleaming planets. Edom's face smiled out from a moon near Planet Jupiter.

Topher hadn't forgotten us. Any of us. "It's my orbit," I told Edom.

Then I saw Traveler. I'd recognize his smart doggy face from a million miles away. I had to turn my head for a few seconds. Finally, I said, "That dog was *not* trouble from Day One."

"That dog," Topher said, "was excellent from Day One."

"What dog?" Edom asked.

"Tell you later," I said. My throat felt like it had an oyster stuck in it—but I'd tell her soon. When you're feeling pathetic, it helps a little to talk with someone who's been through some stuff. "Didn't it rain on you while you were painting?" I managed to ask Topher.

"Sure." Topher put one arm around each of us. "A couple of times, I had to wring my socks out at the end of the day. I'd make myself a cup of tea and curl up in my warm bed and sleep in the next morning."

I nodded. He used to make cups of herbal tea and cocoa when things got tough on the road.

"What would it take to get *you* to sleep, Edom?" Topher asked.

"I don't want to sleep," she said. "When I sleep I forget people's faces."

I knew what she meant—a face that's brilliant in your memory and then fades a tiny bit at a time.

"How about if we paint them?" Topher said. "Your mom and your grandma and Amy-mom. They'll be in my solar system and you won't lose them no matter what."

She studied him, considering. "How will you know what they look like?"

"When I drove up here from California, Amy sent a photo album with me. She was hoping I would get a chance to share it with you."

"Really?" Edom smiled. "Can I see it?"

"Sure. Let's go inside and get it."

While they were gone, I walked over to the tightrope Topher had strung between two trees—like he did wherever we stayed. I kicked my shoes off and used one of the trees to steady myself. I positioned my bare feet carefully, tucking the line under my first two toes. Relax in, Topher had said when he taught me. Empty your mind of everything except feet on the rope.

I walked forward a few steps confidently and gracefully, arms out for balance. Then I started to wobble. I backed up and hung onto the tree.

Someday, maybe I'd have the superpower of understanding exactly what was going on inside of me.

The wind has died down on Planet Jupiter. You feel like an astronaut poking around the dust that's left behind.

I'd never wanted to admit it, but I hated it when Dad left. Even if I knew he was the Prince of Adventure, even if I wanted him to be free, it was still hard. That's why it was so terrible the day Topher left us at Rainbow Farm. He had tried to say good-bye to me, but I was mad, mad, mad! I'd run out of there and hacked blackberries until Orion had made me come inside and had pulled out the thorns with tweezers.

"I'm sorry," he'd said. "That bum."

"You have to promise me we won't *ever* let him back in," I'd said. How could Topher leave us the way Dad had left us? How?

I moved out onto the rope again, using my muscle memory from all the hours Topher and Orion and I practiced.

Topher was one good-bye too many. Little did I know then that Orion was also a good-bye waiting to happen. And now Edom and I had to say good-bye, too?

Suddenly, a thought hit me and I completely lost my balance and had to hop off. Wow. Sometimes it's like an octopus taps you on the shoulder and before you know it, you've changed direction completely. Or you're splat in the ocean with sand in your teeth.

When Topher and Edom came out of the house, Edom sat down with her back against a tree to look at the photo album. I was lying there listening to bamboo in the yard next door brush against itself with a *shh shh* sound. Like being in a tide pool with sunshine angling down and sea stars floating by.

I had started to figure out a few things I needed to say to Topher. He came over. "So." I swallowed hard around what felt like that oyster in my throat. "You think Mom is ready for a new orbit?"

He settled down beside me. "Yes," he said. "Yes, I do."

"Orion definitely is," I said.

"Yep."

"You've been talking to Dad, too, haven't you?" I saw in Topher's face that I was right. I should have known it was Topher and not mole rat vibrations keeping us connected all along.

"What did he say?" I asked.

"He said no problem. He said he loves you all so much."

Dad loved us but he loved adventures too, and . . . a rolling stone gathers no moss.

Orion's voice popped into my head. "Did it ever occur to you, that makes *us* moss?"

Yes. Yes, it does.

I didn't want to be a flicked-off piece of moss. Probably nobody wanted to be flicked-off moss. Including Edom. Including Madam Backyardigan.

"I've got a good idea," I said. "What if we stayed in Portland? All of us—Mom and you and me and maybe Aunt Amy and Edom."

Edom looked up from her album. "Jess would let you ride her skateboard again," she said.

"And you can put a lot of the money we earned into a going-back-to-Ethiopia fund when Aunt Amy is ready," I said. "All but what I saved for Paddy Wagon."

"Do you think you could stand it?" Topher asked. "Having me move in? Settling down at least for a while?"

I turned my head so I could see the elephant's eyes—looking right at me.

"Yes," I said. "Yes, I do."

Chapter Thirty-Eight

Sweetheart, did you bring me silver?
Did you bring me gold?
Or did you come to see me hanging from the gallows cold?
I have brought you silver.
I have brought you gold.
I will bring you anything to keep you from the gallows cold.

So now it was time for a new grand plan.

Topher said he would be done painting the garage soon, and then he'd be moving out of the yellow house. "I hope . . ." He paused and looked at me for a long few minutes. "I hope I'll be moving in with you."

"Do you remember that time we saw the geese and you told us about the upwash?" I asked.

"Uh-huh." He leaned back on his elbows in the grass.

"You said migration can be grueling and the one in front pays a price. And when scientists used GPS, they found out a lot of birds work in pairs and take turns."

Topher sat up and smiled like he saw where I was going with this.

"Yeah," I said. "That's it. That's why you should move in."

"What about the elephant?" Edom asked. "What about Jupiter's orbit?"

"The mural stays behind for the person who hired me to paint it," Topher said. "We can visit it when we want." He tweaked one of Edom's braids. "The guy who owns the little house where you've been living said he's fine renting to us for a while longer. If we want, we can paint faces on those walls, too."

What about Mom? Would she say no again? We should make Topher's proposal a big deal. Maybe with a tiger on a piano or aerial ribbon performers spiraling down purple silk to join Topher on the tightrope.

But even I probably couldn't pull that off.

"One more question," I said to Topher. "Do you think it's true that our hearts start beating in sync to the music we're singing or hearing?"

"So it seems," he said. "And have you read about the new whale song scientists heard when males and females get together that sounds like a deep, low heartbeat?"

"*National Geographic,*" we said in unison.

"Okay," I added. "Then I've got another good idea."

As Topher drove us all toward our house and supper, I explained—and then called Orion. "I have some news," I said when he answered.

He sighed deeply—but maybe it was a happy sigh. "Is this the something good you told me was happening?"

"Not exactly," I said.

The next day, Edom and I went to Jess and Madam Backyardigan's house. "We need singers," I said after I filled them in. "For a flash mob—or at least a flash group of some size. Topher says he knows drummers from Ethos and some buskers including a few from the Portland cello project."

"I'm sure between Grandma and Ms. Evangel and

Victor, we can find everyone in this neighborhood who likes to sing," said Jess.

"Definitely," Madam said.

"I know you don't want people staring at you," I said to Edom.

"That's right," she said. "I don't."

"Help me pick roses," Madam said. "And you can stand right by my chariot and help me hold them."

On the big day, Victor played his part in the plan and took Mom to trade chicken eggs for duck eggs. While they were gone, we all figured out places where we could pretend to be casually standing near the intersection where painted fish gulped on the street—singers and cello players and drummers and three buskers with violins. Cassandra arrived. Madam sat in her chariot. I couldn't see Edom, but I knew she was behind the mobility scooter with her arms full of roses.

"Get ready," Jess called. Topher stepped out of sight behind a tree. I moved to the curb.

But it wasn't Mom who came around the corner. It was Orion, with Zeb and Serena right behind him. "You made it!" I shouted. I barreled into him, almost knocking him down.

"Whoa!" he said. "Dial it back a few decibels."

"Sting me," I said.

"Yeah," he said. "I've missed you, too." He gave me his big coyote grin.

I rubbed Serena's soft ears. "How did you all get here?" I asked.

"Paddy Wagon."

"What?" I poked Orion with my elbow. "You're kidding."

"Nope. It's parked down the block. Right, Zeb?"

Good thing in this neighborhood people could park any old thing any old where.

"I've been working on the engine ever since you left," my brother said. "Topher got me started and Zeb's been helping."

"So we can busk on the beaches on weekends? And have adventures?" I could feel myself smiling big enough to split the sky.

"Yep. If we want." He looked around and grinned at Topher who had moved out beside Madam

Backyardigan and Edom again. "Quite a group you've got here, Jupiter—you and your sixty-seven moons all spinning."

"I know," I said. "And now we can start it all off the way Topher and I most wanted. Here. I'll show you our place."

"Get ready!" Jess called again.

This time, it really was Mom.

As soon as she and Victor came around the corner, Orion and I strode out into the middle of the intersection and let our voices blend together in their spooky sibling way: "Hangman, hangman slack your rope. Slack it for a while." I glanced at Mom. Both of her eyebrows were raised. "What . . ." she started.

The violins joined in as Orion and I kept going: "I think I see my sweetheart coming, traveling many a mile."

I saw Mom catch sight of Edom and Madam Backyardigan. She was definitely starting to understand. All the instruments started playing and the singers moved together and our voices swelled up in sweet, sweet harmony.

"Sweetheart, did you bring me silver?
Sweetheart, did you bring me gold?
Did you bring me anything to keep me from the
    gallows cold?"

Topher moved out from behind the tree and walked toward Mom. He looked so familiar and also a little bit different as he sang:

"I have brought you silver. I have brought you gold."

Before he could finish, Edom got so excited she threw all the roses in the air, and Mom started to laugh. "I'm ready," she said. "Really, really ready."

Everyone cheered when Topher picked Mom up and spun her around. Then Moria made an announcement about the feast she and Danielle had coordinated, working with the locavore restaurant. "They promised no bugs," I whispered to Edom. The whole group—including Mom—sang another love song while Edom and Orion and I stood there holding hands like a three-hearted octopus and Serena ran circles around us.

Orion smiled his loopy grin. "So our cousin really grew on you, huh?"

Yeah, people grew on you. They got stuck on you. In my whole life, whenever I saw a bee, I'd think there goes a pollinator deliciously alive. I wouldn't pass a post office without thinking free boxes! I might pull a weed out of some random person's yard.

Maybe even eat it—with grasshopper on the side.

It was funny what a little moss on Planet Jupiter could do to make things right.

Acknowledgments

Thanks to my singing family—my guitar-and-piano-playing brother and my harmonizing sisters. Making music with you is the shiny spot of my week.

Thanks to Chris Kurtz's third grade class at Abernethy School in Portland for their skateboard demonstrations and for listening to my chapters and treating Jupiter's world with such thoughtful questions and ideas. Chris, you are a prince among men!

Thanks to Ellemae and Noh for reading all the

way through more than once and for your excellent suggestions and resistance.

Thanks to all the adoptive families I've become friends with over the years. Hearing how kids sometimes talk or think about their complicated lives has been huge for this story.

Thanks to my fascinating neighborhood . . . all the ways you are and aren't Portlandia.

Thanks to everyone who asked me questions about Ethiopia—some ignorant and many not—starting when I was seven years old, and for the volunteers and fellow artists who keep me connected as we share a passion for art and reading with young readers in Ethiopia today.

Thanks to the Vermont College of Fine Arts community for fabulous conversations about books and craft. And . . . the singing!

Finally, thanks to all the folk song singers and other performers, including the buskers, who've given me a richer world.